Mountain Girl

The second book of the

Heaven's Mountain trilogy

JACALYN WILSON

Copyright 2011

All rights reserved.

Heaven's Mountain Publishing
5191 Columbus Road
Macon, Georgia 31206

ISBN-13: 9781494355111
ISBN-10: 1494355116

Prologue

My Fair Mountain Girl

In this valley so low, when twilight descends,
Only darkness and clouds 'round me swirl
But she's there just beyond, and she beckons me come,
Just the wisp of my fair mountain girl.

When the sun shone warm and the hills were green,
How we danced through the blue flowers wild!
As I followed her then, I must follow her now,
My beloved, my dear mountain child.

O my fair mountain girl, come again to the hills,
Pray return to this desolate world.
Let us traipse through the woods as we did long ago,
O my lost one, my fair mountain girl.

In the winter so bleak, when the winds do chill,
And the hearth-fire warms not the soul,
I hear her sweet voice in the wail of the wind,
And my tears fill a bottomless hole.

O, the darkness, it swallows and will not restore;
The mist and the fog, they prevail.
Still her memory lingers, and carries me on
In my quest for the dear mountain girl.

O my fair mountain girl, come again to the hills,
Pray return to this desolate world.
Let us traipse through the woods as we did long ago,
O my lost one, my fair mountain girl.

O the dear one, my fair mountain girl.

One

Tuesday
August 18, 1970

Clare sat straight up in bed. From the direction of the kitchen came the sound of pots and pans rolling around on the linoleum. She squinted her eyes to peer at the old alarm clock on the bedside table. Four-thirty. That was only slightly better than four a.m. two mornings ago. With a resigned sigh, she threw her legs over the side of the bed, pushed her arms through the sleeves of her housecoat and scuffed her way into the kitchen of the boarding house.

From his position on the floor, scrambling to corral the cookware, James looked up with a sheepish expression. "I'm so sorry. I was going to get breakfast started for you. I keep forgetting about all the pans and utensils hanging over the cook table.... Looks like I'd remember by now."

"It's all right." She stifled a yawn, then fibbed, "It was almost time for me to get up anyway."

Ruefully he smiled and shook his head. "No, it wasn't. But thank you for being so gracious about it."

Clare got the ground coffee from the pantry and began to measure it into the basket on the large percolator. After hanging the last pan, James leaned back against the counter and crossed one foot over the other. He ought not to be so fine-looking, she thought. Lean body, salt and pepper hair, and the baby, baby, baby-blue-est eyes she'd ever seen., and here she was, having to pretend she wasn't the least bit attracted to him, just because she was the proprietor of this boarding house and it was up to her to maintain the strictest decorum between any male boarder and herself.

Besides, regardless of her feelings, James wasn't ready for a relationship with anybody. Even though it had been two years since his full pardon and release from prison for a murder he didn't commit, Clare knew it was still a struggle for him to live and think as a free man, with choices and options and opportunities. The regimen of an institutionalized existence had become deeply ingrained after almost thirty years.

Interestingly enough, his incarceration was no deterrent to the local females who were interested in the handsome preacher. The thought of all those older ladies in church chasing him like a greased pig at a county fair caused a giggle to bubble out, but she quickly covered it with a snort, and cleared her throat. "Morning stuff in my throat," she explained, pointing at her neck.

James unwound his legs and rubbed his hands together. "Can I start the sausage – or bacon – for you? Or is it pancakes today? Want me to start them?"

Clare looked doubtfully at the clock on the wall which said a quarter to five. More than two hours until serving time. "N-n-n-no. It's still too early. Why don't you fix yourself some coffee, and maybe get a piece of pie to hold you until breakfast? Come back about six-fifteen and you can help me cook if you want to." He looked a little disappointed, so she added, "You're a lot of help, you know."

"Thanks," he answered. "I'll just wait on the coffee, then go out on the porch for my devotions. You going back to bed?"

"Yeah. I really need that extra hour of beauty sleep," she admitted as she walked toward her private rooms off of the kitchen. "Make yourself at home, James."

Two

There's a nip in the air this morning, thought James, cold enough that a sweater would feel good as he read his Bible out here on the screened porch. Still, that little comfort didn't seem important enough to warrant a trip to his room upstairs. It would be hot within a few hours anyway, and unpleasant temperatures were one of the things to which he had grown accustomed while in prison. There were so many things over which he had no control in that place that he had no choice but to tamp down his natural desire to manage his own life. Now that he was a free man, he found himself still doing many things automatically, without considering that he could choose, if he preferred, to do them in an entirely different way. It was something he prayed about. Every morning, he asked God to wash from him all those unseen effects of prison life. He knew he was innocent, a victim of unfair circumstances, but he also knew that he was not the same confident young man who had entered those locked gates so long ago.

During all that time in prison, he had always been at peace, secure in the knowledge that, in spite of his circumstances, God was using him for good. Even now he had no doubt that his prison ministry should continue, or that he should pastor a church again, so his work was not the source of the uncertainty he frequently felt. There was just an indefinable sense of not belonging, not fitting in this modern, liberated world into which he had been thrown. To re-state an old saying, maybe it was simply a case of "you can take the man out of the prison, but you can't take the prison out of the man". Habits learned over decades were not easily broken.

Like this morning. That embarrassing scene in the kitchen with Clare. He wished he could stop waking up so early. For twenty eight years he had been roused at four a.m. so he could work the breakfast shift in the prison's kitchen and that old prison schedule still woke him most mornings. But some mornings, like today, it was the dream that woke him up.

With only slight variations, the dream was always the same. He and Betty (his wife who died of cancer while he was in prison) were on a picnic in a small grassy clearing, up near the highest point of Heaven's Mountain. They were young and carefree and very much in love. Betty was teasing him and they were both laughing. He chased her as she flitted from tree to tree, hiding behind one, then another, going ever deeper into the woods. As it grew darker the distance between them increased. The fog settling into the hollows dampened his senses, and he could no longer see her or hear her. For a long time he searched and called for her, running until he was breathless. Then he saw her, or at least a wisp of her, drifting amidst the fog, but he couldn't reach her. Every time he got close, the apparition would glide even further away. In his dream the sadness and frustration were crushing. He wanted her to return to him. He wanted things to be the way they were before. He wanted his old life back.

Three

"Oh, foot!" huffed Grace. "Ethan, would you please come and tie these shoes for me?" Having gained a considerable amount of weight during the first eight months of her pregnancy, Grace had decided to temporarily put away her sweet little Pappagallo flats, which had become uncomfortably tight, and wear her Keds for the duration. She hadn't counted on the difficulty involved in getting past her tummy to get to the shoestrings.

"Coming! I'm coming, sweetheart," her husband called out from the kitchen. Perched on the side of the bed, Grace leaned back on her elbows and smiled contentedly. In the husband department, she was hugely blessed and she knew it. Ethan was about as perfect as an imperfect man could be. He was tender and kindhearted and honest, and so good to help around the house, not to mention how supportive he was of her career. Her unabashed love for him slammed right into her raging pregnant hormones and the waterworks began.

"Honey, what's the matter?" Ethan came to her and gently put his arms around her. "Why are you crying?"

"I don't know!" she wailed. "I'm just so happy, and I love you so much!"

Bewildered, again, Ethan resigned himself to the fact that he was not going to understand what was going on in his wife's head and went on to the business at hand. He slid the first leg up into his lap and began tying the sneaker. "What are you going to do today?" he asked.

"I'm going in to work this morning," she hiccupped. "Joe wants me to work on the house fire story. Want to meet me back here for lunch? We've got some leftover ham; we could make sandwiches."

"I think I could manage that. Did I tell you I was meeting with someone from Harry Carroll's organization?"

"That traveling evangelist guy?"

"Yeah, that's the one. He heard me speak at the rally in Gainesville back in June. They want to talk to me about getting involved in their program."

Grace was pushing herself up off the bed. "Really? That's pretty flattering, isn't it? I mean, he must have been impressed with you, to want you to join his team."

"Well, he hasn't asked me yet. He just wants to talk."

Grace's eyebrows drew together and she ran her tongue across her front teeth. "But Ethan, I don't know if I want you to be traveling, especially not now, with a baby due in only one month. And after the baby gets here – I don't want to be left alone while you're out of town…" The tears began flowing again.

"Aw, gee….." and he pulled her back into his arms.

Four

Today was Tuesday, and on Tuesdays James always spent the entire day at the prison, where he led a chapel service, followed by a Bible study, with the rest of the day spent in counseling work. He had already done his preparation for today, but since he had extra time this morning, due to getting up early again, he spent some time working on the following week's Bible study and sermon.

The next time he checked his watch it was ten after six. Time to help Clare with breakfast. As he packed up his Bible and notebooks he noticed, with some surprise, that he actually felt a sense of happy anticipation of the task ahead. Not so strange really, considering how much he enjoyed cooking. And of course, Clare was….well, she was rather captivating, in a homey, comfortable way. Like a sweet, amusing sister, always stirring up some mischief and fun. He put aside his thoughts and hurried on to the kitchen.

In less than an hour they were putting food out on the buffet table and shortly thereafter, the first of the boarders shuffled in. Though they probably wouldn't have appreciated the comparison, breakfast at the boarding house reminded James of mealtime at the prison and, as was his longstanding practice, he made it a point to give each person at the table an encouraging word with which to begin their day.

Clare took her breakfast in the kitchen so that she could replenish the breakfast bar as needed. On one of her rounds she stopped to refresh his coffee. "Thanks for the help this morning," she said.

"Always a pleasure," he replied sincerely. He found himself watching her as she bustled about, seeing to everyone's needs, always cheerful and kind, ready to laugh at their jokes or share one herself. She was really quite special, he thought.

In the prison mess hall, they were allowed exactly thirty minutes to eat breakfast, so when his internal clock signaled that time was up, James couldn't help himself. He had to get up and leave.

The prison was some twenty miles away, but James didn't mind the drive. After years of having little or no say-so over his daily activities, to have control of a vehicle and choose his own destination was no small thing. He doubted he would ever take those freedoms for granted, no matter how long he lived.

To top it all off, he got to drive his own truck, one that he owned free and clear. James was proud of his '58 Chevy truck. True, it was nowhere near as nice as the models they had nowadays, but he had paid for it himself, with the money he earned doing odd carpentry jobs, and it was definitely luxurious when compared with the old Ford open cab pickup he drove before going to prison. Ethan had done his best to get his father to let him help pay for the Chevy pickup, but James was glad now that he hadn't given in.

His needs were simple, which was fortunate, because his income was meager indeed. At the encouragement and insistence of the old Heaven's Mountain Church members, he had accepted the challenge of re-opening the little church near the mountain's top and resuming his pastoral role. In keeping with its size, the congregation could offer only a small salary, but it was enough to cover his room and board at the boarding house. So that stipend, along with the occasional carpentry job, was sufficient to meet his basic needs, leaving him ample time to continue his ministry at the prison, a work that was close to his heart.

James had visited the facility almost every week in the last two years, but driving past the guard shack and then going through the visitors' checkpoints never failed to cause a moment - just a heartbeat - of minor anxiety. It was always a relief to enter the classroom that served as the chapel.

Today, as was his routine, James readied his notes, placed a Bible on the seat of each chair, then picked up a stack of hymnals to distribute. When he heard the sound of a guard unlocking the door, he turned to see Bo Lucas enter. This was the man whose confession had resulted in James' pardon. They had had many long talks since then and had become good friends. Though James' hands were full, they managed to exchange a hearty hug.

"Here, let me get those for you, Preacher," said Bo, holding out his hands for the books. .

"Bo! I'm glad you're here early," said James as he handed over the songbooks. "I can use some help getting everything set up."

Bo laid all of the hymnals in the seats of the folding chairs then, sticking his hands deep in his pockets, came back up to the wooden lectern. "The guard let me come a few minutes early, Preacher, 'cause I wanted to ask you about something." Staring out the barred windows, Bo began, "You know I've got a little girl."

"Yes. Sophia, isn't it?"

"That's right. Sophia. We call her Sophie."

"I like that." James waited patiently for him to continue.

Bo faced him squarely now. "Sophie's got a birthday party this weekend. Five. She'll be five years old." Bo cleared his throat as emotion threatened to overcome him.

James put his hand on Bo's shoulder. "What can I do for you?"

"I need somebody to go to her birthday party and represent me. My boy Billy is usually really good about seeing to these things for me, but you know he goes to college, and this week he has to go to summer camp with the baseball team. He's got a baseball scholarship – he's really good, but anyway, that's why I need someone."

"Of course. I can do that. Katrina won't mind, will she?" Sophie's parents, Katrina and Bo, had gotten married soon after Bo was sent to prison. James had performed the ceremony.

"No, she'll be happy to have you come, Preacher. And I've got twenty-five dollars saved up, for you to get Sophie a present that's just from me. A surprise. Think you can handle that?"

James chuckled. "Are you sure you trust me to buy a present for a five year old girl? I don't know anything about what they like."

"Well….I don't want to be any trouble….."

"Bo, I'm just kidding! I'll ask Grace, my daughter-in-law. She'll know exactly what to do."

Five

"Yes-sir-ee, bob! Them womenfolk, when they're with child, they have some strange cravings, and it ain't all for food, let me tell you." Diggy was clearly in hog heaven, with Ethan as a captive audience of one. The young preacher had slid into an empty booth at the diner, only to have the old jailer slip in beside him. Now his only escape routes were under the table, over the table, or climbing over Diggy.

Ethan tried again, saying, "Diggy, I'm supposed to meet someone, so…"

"Now, you know you have to watch her feet, don't you?"

"Whose feet?"

"Your wife's feet. In case they start swelling up."

"Well, I…"

"'Cause that's right dangerous. 'Course I already knew all there was to know about that, but I read an article on it last time I was at the doctor's office."

"I haven't actually…"

"Things can happen to that new little baby, too…"

"Grace is the one that…"

"So don't dilly-dally when it's time to get that girl to the hospital either, if you don't want to have to hand-deliver.…" The tinkle of the bell over the entrance door gave Diggy a reason to pause and take a gander at the newcomer. Ethan knew by the grey suit and tie that this must be someone from the evangelist's organization, so he took advantage of the sudden quiet to say calmly but firmly, "Would you let me out, Diggy?"

Diggy looked from Ethan to the stranger and back again. "Oh. Oh, sure, Preacher," he said as he slid out.

"See you later, Diggy." Holding out his hand, Ethan approached the gentleman. "Good morning. I'm Ethan MacEwen."

"Ethan. Nice to meet you. I'm Donald Kendrick. Harry couldn't make it today. He sends his regrets. He asked me to meet with you instead."

"Pleasure to meet you, Donald. How about if we sit back there in the corner? It should be a little quieter."

Over coffee, Mr. Kendrick discussed the various programs their organization maintained, stopping to answer Ethan's many enthusiastic questions along the way.

"So, we need someone in this area to represent the Path of Grace Ministry. We – Harry and I – were hoping you would consider it. We were both very impressed by the presentation you gave at that meeting in Gainesville." The dark-suited minister, second in command over the national program, was watching Ethan closely, obviously trying to gauge his response.

Ethan took a deep breath and shook his head in wonder. "I'm truly humbled. To even be considered by an organization like yours, not to mention being singled out by Harry, knowing what kind of man he is, it's just…amazing to me!"

"You've got much to give, Ethan, and we would consider ourselves fortunate to have you on our team. Now, we're growing by leaps and bounds, therefore this position is going to require more time, more travel, more dedication, than ever before. You would be responsible for the entire state, reporting to the southeast director in Dallas, Texas, so you would be in Dallas two to four days each month. You would also need to meet regularly with each of the ten district leaders in this state, at least once a month. When we have our spring tour and our fall tour, you would need to travel with us at least part of that time."

"Wow. That's a lot of time away from home. I don't know if I can do that. My wife is due in one month with our first baby…"

"I understand. Just give it some thought, talk to your wife about it, and, most important, pray about it."

"I will," Ethan assured him. "When do you need an answer?"

"You've got one month."

Six

At about that same time, Grace was poking her head around the kitchen door at the boarding house. "Clare! Are you here?"

From within the house, a high-pitched "cartoon character" voice sang out, "Nobody here but us 'house mouses', ma'am!" Grace crossed the kitchen and there was Clare, standing at the top of the back stairs, with a broom in one hand and a mouse trap in the other, a mouse trap currently occupied by a fat gray rodent.

Grace put her hand somewhere in the neighborhood of where her hip used to be and shook her head slowly from side to side. "Clare, I have come to the conclusion that you're about a bubble off of plumb, as my Granny Annie has been known to say from time to time. I used to think you reminded me of my mother, but you're in a league all your own, girl."

Tramping down the stairs, Clare sniffed in mock offense. "Well! Somebody has to be the mouse catcher around here!" She placed the trap, mouse and all, in a paper bag and laid it by the trash can. "I'll take care of Mickey's friend later. So, what brings you to the asylum today, snookums? Jiminy Cricket, you're getting huge!"

"Tell me about it! Ethan had to tie my shoes for me this morning." Grace walked the distance of the long kitchen counter, checking out all of the baked goods. "Ooh, Clare, can I have some of this cherry pie?"

"Only if you drink a glass of milk with it," bossed Clare. She filled a glass with milk and cut a generous piece of pie for her friend. After pouring herself a cup of coffee, she sat down beside Grace at the kitchen table. "So, what brings you here today? Don't you work anymore?"

"Ha. Ha. Yes, I do. But I had a few minutes to kill, and I haven't seen you in ages, so here I am." Grace used her fork to scrape up the last smidgen of cherry syrup, then licked her lips. She giggled. "Actually, I just came to get some of this delicious pie. You and my momma *are* the same when it comes to making pies."

Clare put her arm around Grace's shoulder and squeezed. "You can come anytime. You and Ethan both should visit James sometimes. I know he comes to your house, but you're welcome to come here, too. I have that little sunroom; you'd have plenty of privacy."

"Yeah, we need to do that. Speaking of James, any indications of.... anything?"

Clare shook her head sadly. "We get along just great. I'm sure he likes me, as far as that goes. But there's never even a hint of anything more from him. And I'm *real* careful not to let my feelings show."

"Hmm. Maybe it's time for Plan B."

Clare rolled her eyes. "Oh, heavens to Betsy, what are you gonna' get me into now?"

Serious now, Grace spoke softly. "You know the disciple in the Bible that had no guile? That's how James is. Maybe you just need to let him know how you feel. What's the worst that could happen?"

Seven

*E*ver since James had come to stay at the boarding house, he and Clare had fallen into the routine of playing various board games every Tuesday night. Though his formal education far exceeded hers, she was well-read and intelligent enough that they were well matched as competitors. A pleasant rivalry ensued with the end result being that, through all the teasing and ribbing that was dished out, they got to know each other well and became fast friends.

"That is not a word, James MacEwen." Clare looked at the scrabble board again. "Is it?"

"Where's the dictionary? Not the little one, the big one." He flipped the pages until he found what he was looking for. "See, there it is. Menology."

"What is that? The study of men?"

"No. It's an ecclesiastical calendar of months."

"Oh, good grief. I'm not gonna play with you any more," she teased. "You know too many words."

"You're no slacker yourself, Miss Morgan. Wasn't it just a couple of weeks ago you used the word "limn", a word which I had never seen in my life."

"It was in a romance novel I read a long time ago," she admitted as she began packing up the game pieces. "Anyway, you just wait. Next time, we're going to play gin rummy, and I am warning you – I am very good at gin."

"I'll be ready," he promised. "Oh, by the way, I had a great idea today."

"You did?" she feigned surprise. "Well, do tell."

"Since I can't seem to break the habit of waking at four a.m., and since I seem to owe you some extra sleep to make up for all the mornings I wake you….." He paused for effect.

"Well?" she prodded.

"Why don't you write out your breakfast menu each week and leave it out for me? On the mornings I come down early, I'll cook breakfast and have it all ready when you get up. You can sleep a little longer, or just relax in your rooms for an extra hour."

"I can't let you do that, James," she protested.

"Why not? You don't think I can handle it?"

"Well, sure… I guess…"

"Actually, Clare, you'd be doing me a favor. I kind of miss working in the kitchen. You know, after so many years, cooking breakfast every morning in prison."

"But you're in the kitchen helping me all the time."

"It's not the same as doing it all myself. Come on, what do you say? Will you write out the menu for me?"

How could she refuse, with those sweet blue eyes pleading with her? "Okay, if you insist. Just don't make the coffee too strong," she cautioned.

He grinned. "Yes, ma'am."

Eight

Wednesday
August 19

There. She heard it again. Clare was in the third floor bathroom in the middle of the morning, cleaning. All the boarders were gone about their business for the day, so aside from her scrubbing, the house was quiet and still. Except for that little scritch-scratching noise coming from behind the wall in the bathroom. She knew it had to be another mouse.

She didn't like the nasty little varmints, but neither was she afraid of them. With her usual confidence and determination to deal with whatever the old house might throw at her, she hurried downstairs to the supply closet to get the mousetraps.

Then, armed with the traps and a bowl of bait (peanut butter and pieces of pecans), she marched right back upstairs and opened the door to the attic.

Measuring off in her mind the distance from the attic door to the area behind the upstairs bath, she immediately saw that she was going to have to climb out into the open space, beyond the part of the attic that was floored with plywood, onto the support beams, in order to reach the bathroom wall.

"Oh, rats!" she said, then giggled at the unintended pun. "No offense, Mickey or Minnie or whoever."

Later, as she looked back on this little episode, she would admit to herself that she should have waited until she had help. But at the moment, she was feeling empowered and strong, the one-woman handyman landlord capable of handling every maintenance problem and rental emergency all on her own.

And so she stepped confidently out on the wide support beam, careful to avoid the swaths of insulation tucked between the beams. The further she went, the more she had to stoop over to allow for the slope of the roof.

Stopping in the area of the bathroom wall, she got down on her knees to set the two traps. She baited the first one and set it out, pushing it up against the wall. She could see several holes gnawed in the plywood, where the mouse was probably making his daily rounds. In fact, the rodent probably had an easy time of it, because now that she looked more closely, the boards looked rotten, maybe due to dampness in the bathroom.

She wanted to set the other trap a little further down the wall. It was going to be difficult to access, due to a six inch rafter slanting down, blocking her way. Still on her knees, she inched down the beam, ducking her head under the rafter. She lifted up a little too soon, however, for something sharp cut into her back and she could feel her shirt caught on whatever it was. An old nail, perhaps.

A gentle tug did no good at all. The fabric wasn't releasing or tearing. She tried again, a little harder. The problem was, she was bent over in such an awkward position, she couldn't put any muscle into it. She didn't especially want to take her shirt off, so she looked around for another option.

Turning just slightly, she reached out for the bathroom wall and grabbed a stud with one hand. Bracing her feet and pushing off, she pulled herself toward the stud as hard and fast as she could. The fabric gave way more easily than she'd expected and the unchecked momentum sent her straight into the rotten boards, which buckled easily under the pressure. Her head, shoulders and one arm slipped right between two studs and she found herself staring at the tile floor of the bathroom, blinking hard to keep the plaster dust out of her eyes.

Mountain Girl

Her body weight had wedged her down into a tight fit against the remaining wall, but she could move a little. Using her feet to gain a bit of traction, she managed to push herself an inch or two back into the attic when she heard footsteps on the stairs.

She stopped moving, hoping that whoever it was, they hadn't heard the commotion.

"Clare?" It was James. Of course, it had to be James, the person she would least like to see her like this. "Is that you? Are you all right?"

Golly, couldn't she ever catch a break? Might as well 'fess up now. "It's me. I'm in here, in the bathroom." She corrected herself, "More or less."

"May I come in?"

"May as well." She stopped herself. "No, wait. NO! Not until you absolutely promise that you will never tell a living soul what you're about to see."

He didn't say anything for a few seconds, obviously weighing the possible ramifications of the promise he was about to make.

Finally he murmured, "I promise…I guess."

"Come on in." She saw the door swing slowly open, first revealing a thatch of salt and pepper hair, followed by just his eyes. He was holding the door, covering the rest of his face, but the eyes told the story all by themselves. From serious concern to amused smile to stifled laughter.

She squeezed her own eyes shut for a moment in sheer embarrassment. When they opened again, they were shining with her own suppressed merriment. "Okay," she choked out. "You've seen me." A chuckle came snorting out. "Now, get in here and help me out of this!"

To his credit, he only laughed a little, not nearly as much as Clare, who thoroughly appreciated the hilarity of the situation, and kept dissolving into weak-kneed giggles, rendering herself totally useless in the extrication process. James would just hold her up until the laughter subsided, and then they would begin again with the pushing and pulling.

When all of Clare was back on the attic side of the wall, James came through from the other side into the attic.

"Need any help?"

"No, I think I can handle it from here. Just let me gather up my things." It was at that point, when she felt an unfettered breeze across her back, that she realized the back of her shirt was no longer there, and she wondered what state of disarray she must have been in while stuck in the wall.

Oh, well. They were both adults. Mature, reasonable adults with plenty of common sense. A little more subdued now, Clare walked out of the attic in a dignified, grown-up manner, moving sedately past James who was holding the door open for her.

But then, as she passed, James sniffed and studied her hair. "Clare? Wait, there's something in your hair…" His fingers reached for a small brown glob, but stopped before touching it. "It looks like……peanut butter?"

She wished she could drop straight through the floor. "Mmm. Yes, peanut butter. Don't ask," she demanded, her tone brooking no argument.

"Sure," he said meekly. Then, "Uh, Clare. That hole in the wall…? Would you like me to…you know….?"

"Oh, just fix it, for goodness sake!" Her feet were clipping along down the next set of stairs when she added, "D'you like my banana pudding, James?"

"Yes! I love your banana pudding."

"If you tease me about this, I will never make banana pudding for you again." She turned her head around and he knew she was joking.

"It might be worth losing banana pudding forever – to get to tell this story," he shot back.

"Aw, shucks. I forgot for a moment that you were a preacher, and preachers just *love* a good story. Well, just don't use it in a sermon, okay?"

"I can't make any promises."

"Well, come on then, have a cup of coffee with me, and we'll see if we can't come to some mutually beneficial arrangement." Clare stopped to let him catch up with her and put her arm around his waist. She giggled again, obviously remembering the ridiculousness of the fiasco. "We wouldn't want to ruin a great friendship over a little thing like this, would we?"

Mountain Girl

He laughed, too, and she wondered if she would ever see anything more in his eyes than friendship. If friendship was what God had in mind for them, then she would just have to treasure and be thankful for that friendship but she couldn't help hoping that someday there would be more.

Nine

"Grace, do you have the school board meeting piece ready?"

"Joe, I put that on your desk yesterday!"

"Oh. Oh, yeah, I remember now." Joe rubbed his forehead. "I think I'm so excited about taking a week off, I can't keep my mind on work today."

"That's okay, boss," she teased. "We will overlook your absent-mindedness because we are so looking forward to playing all next week while you're gone!"

Joe had been walking to the back, but he turned around, tipped his glasses down his nose, and sent Grace a doubtful look. "As if that could be true! You poor working stiffs will have to exert yourselves twice as hard just to stay afloat, without me here!"

"Maybe," she conceded. "Hey, Joe, anything new about the development company that's been making all that noise about a resort?"

"The Stockton Corporation. You covered the county commissioners' meeting where they introduced themselves and their proposed project, so you probably know more than I do. You saw how our officials jumped at the chance to bring more revenue into the county. I think the project could garner a lot of support, as long as everything's on the up and up."

Jacalyn Wilson

"Are we going to do an "in-depth" on it?"

"Absolutely. But I'm waiting until their representative gets here. In fact, you may have to handle that next week while I'm gone."

"Will do, Boss."

Ten

Thursday
August 20, 1970

Clare's ponytail was no longer perky. As of Thursday morning the week had officially become a maintenance nightmare. After a stint of practically standing on her head plunging the stopped-up toilet on the second floor, her coiffure was now disheveled and decidedly lopsided, which was unfortunate, because at that very moment a handsome gentleman was standing on her front porch preparing to knock.

Knock! Knock! Clare's head popped up and she huffed a time or two to blow her hair out of her eyes. When that didn't do the job, she threw down the plunger, stripped off her rubber gloves and swiped the hair to one side. A quick look in the mirror was no comfort at all. Her face was red and running wet with perspiration. Oh, well. It was probably George, the postman, needing to hand deliver a large package for one of the boarders, a fairly regular occurrence, and George had probably seen her looking worse than this when she was doing yard work. With a square of toilet paper she blotted her nose and eyes then headed downstairs. She never even noticed the big dark wet circle right in the middle of her shirt, where she had splashed toilet water during all that vigorous plunging.

Her first thought, when she opened the door and saw the stranger, was how "smooth" he was. Everything about him was smooth. His abundant dark hair, with distinguished gray highlights at the temples, was smoothly combed down. The material of his expensive tailored suit was smooth and unwrinkled. His fancy dress shoes were gleaming. And even though he was obviously not a young man, his face was smooth, like a baby's. In fact, this fellow looked as if he had just stepped off the silver screen. It didn't happen often to the loquacious Clare, but she was impressed to the point of being speechless.

"Good afternoon," said the gentleman, with a slight bow. He smiled in a friendly manner and waited a few seconds for a response. When none came, he continued, "My name is Edward English. I understand that you take boarders?"

Oh, Lordy, she thought. She took hold of herself enough to squeak, "Yes."

At her short answer, he seemed a bit bemused, but recovered his aplomb and inquired politely, "Would you happen to have a room available at this time? I would need to stay for three weeks."

Clare was ready this time. "Yes, sir. I have a lovely upstairs room with a double bed. Would you like to see it?"

"Yes, please." Mr. English followed Clare up the stairs to the large sunny bedroom with its own bath. The décor was a combination of French country and American country, charming and warm in blues and butter yellows. "This will do nicely," he commented. "I wasn't expecting such generous amenities. I have to work on my reports at night, so I'll make good use of this desk." He ran his hand across the top of an oversized armchair. "The workmanship on this chair is exceptional. I don't think I've ever seen one quite like it before."

"Try it out," she urged. "You just melt into those chairs, they're so comfortable. Jed Liles makes those chairs," she said proudly.

"This is a local craftsman?"

"Yes, sir."

"Will you introduce me? My sister owns several furniture stores. I think she'd be very interested."

"I'd be happy to take you over there one day while you're here. He has a shop about ten miles out of town."

Mountain Girl

In the course of giving Mr. English a guided tour of the rest of the house, Clare learned that he worked for the Stockton Corporation, a property development company headquartered in New York. The company was planning to develop a resort area in the north Georgia mountains and Mr. English was here to acquire sales contracts for the land.

By the time Mr. English signed the guest register, Clare was no longer overwhelmed by her new boarder's sophisticated appearance. Though his manners were old-worldly formal, the courtesy was of the genuine kind, that made the other person's comfort the highest priority, so she found herself forgetting any differences in their circumstances, to simply enjoy a conversation with a very pleasant man. A very pleasant *handsome* man.

She was feeling very smart and sophisticated herself as she went back upstairs to resume her work on the toilet. It only took one horrified glance in the mirror – wild hair, red face and blotched shirt - to burst that delicious bubble and send her plummeting back to the real world with a thud.

Eleven

Well, they smell the same, thought James, taking another whiff from the bag containing the two chili dogs he had just purchased from the old pool hall on the square. *If they taste the way they did thirty years ago, I'll be a happy man.* He had finished a porch repair that morning then on a whim had stopped in at Finlay's Billiards to pick up some lunch.

Since the mid August heat had eased off somewhat he got the dogs and a Pepsi to go. The City Park was just a block off the square with picnic tables and lots of shade from big hardwoods, so he turned the truck in that direction.

There was no one else around, not even any little tykes on the playground. The single lane road split, and he took the right fork leading to a gazebo which was situated by a cheerful little brook. A nice, quiet place to enjoy his lunch.

He sat down at a wooden bench only a few feet from the water, gave thanks, and almost swooned at the aroma when he opened the bag of food. This was going to be good, even if it meant certain heartburn an hour from now.

He was just about to take his first bite when a rattle-trap pickup truck came wheezing down the hill and lurched into the parking space next to his.

A rough looking fellow got out and slammed the door. Even in the summer heat, he had on a flannel shirt, open over a graying tee shirt and worn blue jeans hanging low enough that a streak of his potbelly showed though. Cowboy boots that looked like they might have been expensive at one time peeked out below the ragged hem of the jeans. As if on a mission, he headed straight for James.

Beginning to feel a little apprehensive, James put the chili dog down. This didn't feel right.

"You the preacher?" asked the man.

"Yes, sir. I am a preacher," James answered.

"The one that got let out of jail a while back?"

"Yes. Can I help you with something?"

"You can't help me with nothin'!" he exclaimed, then took a moment to draw up the tobacco juice in his mouth and shoot it between his teeth to a spot a few inches from the preacher's feet.

In the meantime, James was feeling completely bewildered. He'd never seen the fellow before, but thought it best to sit quietly and see what he had to say. It didn't take long.

Moving to within a few feet of where James sat on the bench, he started again. "I don't know who you think you are, goin' around fillin' my boy's head full of drivel, but it's gonna stop right now or I'm gonna turn you inside out."

Were it not for the fact that James had heard plenty of this kind of blustering bully talk while in prison, he might have indeed panicked, but since he was all too familiar with this kind of ruffian, he responded calmly. "I'm not sure who your son is, sir, but I don't force anybody to listen."

That seemed to infuriate him even more. He pointed his finger at James, and barked, "My son's serving his time like a man, but you're turning him into a mealy-mouth fool with all that Jesus-love stuff. Now, I'm warning you, you stay away from him, or I'll be paying you another visit, and it won't be near as nice and pleasant as this one."

Having evidently said his piece, the man began to stomp up the hill to his truck. Though he didn't want to get the fellow started again,

James thought it the wiser course to find out the identity of the son, so he called out, "Who is your son?"

The man turned and growled, "Darrell Woody is my boy and I'd best not hear that you've gone near him again."

James watched until the old truck was out of sight, then looked down at his cold, greasy chili dogs. So much for gastronomic pleasures from the past. Regretfully, he tossed the food in the edge of the woods for the wildlife, and took a long swig of the lukewarm Pepsi before throwing it in the trash.

Twelve

The summer days were growing shorter, with autumn waiting in the wings, but the days were still long enough that after supper, most nights, James could work on his own special project – repairing the old Lucas place. Following his pardon, Bo and Billy Lucas had given him ten acres and the house, located near the summit of Heaven's Mountain. His hope was to have the remodeling completed by the end of the year and move in as soon as possible.

After hurrying through Clare's dinner of lasagna and garlic bread, he picked up Ethan on the way out of town. Grace waved at them from the kitchen door as James backed out of the driveway. "So, how is Grace feeling?" he asked his son.

Ethan gave a short laugh and shook his head. "Physically, I believe she's doing great, but, Dad, I don't know what's going on in her head!" He turned to look at James. "Did Mom get all weepy and kind of weird when she was pregnant?"

"Oh, yeah. I remember that part very well. Especially the day your mother got so mad at me for being late for supper."

"Why? What did she say?"

"Oh, she didn't say anything. She took all my clothes and threw them down in the well, then she started walking to her momma's house - thirteen miles away."

"My sweet little soft-spoken momma did that? I'd never have believed that about Mom," he chuckled, shaking his head. "Well, then. I guess you do know what I'm talking about. But, what I want to know is, how long is this going to last?"

"Oh, it'll get better. At least by the time the child starts school," said James with an almost straight face.

"Okay, okay. Some things aren't meant to be joked about, Dad," quipped Ethan, looking askance at the older man.

They were quiet as the '58 Chevy truck wound around the tight curves going up the incline toward the mountaintop. A half-mile from the summit James turned left, down a rugged one lane drive.

Ethan commented, "Things will be easier anyway, after the baby comes and Grace isn't working any more."

"Oh, so she's not planning on going back to the newspaper? Not even part-time?" They reached the end of the lane with the small cottage now sitting right in front of them. James turned off the truck.

"No, she'll be at home with the baby, and I'm really looking forward to that," said Ethan as they went in the house. "All right, what are we going to work on today?"

James led him to the bathroom, where the floor was rotted and needed to be replaced. "Let's work on this floor this evening. I think we might even be able to finish it before it gets dark." They worked in silence, pulling up decaying boards, then James opened the bathroom window and began throwing the planks outside. "Hey, was it this week you were supposed to meet with Harry Carroll's man?"

"Tuesday morning, yeah."

"And..?

"I thought it went very well. They offered me the position of state director. I have a month to think it over and give them my decision." He handed James a broken board. "Their organization is impressive and it's an honor to be asked, but there's a lot of travel involved." He

Mountain Girl

hesitated. "Grace will definitely not like that and I'm not looking forward to discussing it with her either."

"Hey, now," his dad cajoled. "Grace is a reasonable person, son."

"Yeah, under normal circumstances, but right now she's in the clutches of some kind of temporary pregnancy insanity," joked Ethan. "And you'd better not repeat what I just said to anybody, especially Grace!" he said, shaking his finger in fun at his father.

"I won't. But seriously, Grace is a woman of strong faith, Ethan. She'll try to discern the Lord's will and follow it."

"You're right, I know. All kidding aside, I've been praying that God will make it clear to me, whatever his will might be about this job offer. I'd appreciate it if you'd pray for me, too."

"Every day, son. Every day."

Thirteen

Friday
August 21

When Ethan answered the door and James heard Grace crying in the background, he knew that it was not the time to ask for help choosing Sophie's birthday present. He didn't even go in the house, just gave Ethan a sympathetic smile and shrug, then beat a hasty retreat back to the safe haven of his pickup truck. What was he to do now, he wondered. It was only two days until Sophie's birthday, and he had counted on being able to turn the whole responsibility over to Grace.

He put the key in the ignition and froze as a feeling of panic swept over him. He started breathing hard. What was he going to do? He couldn't let Bo down, but he had no experience with this part of "normal" life. In a totally uncalled for reaction, he felt desperate and anxious that he wouldn't be able to meet everyone's expectations. What was wrong with him? Where was this feeling coming from? A little girl's birthday present was no reason to get so agitated yet his heart was beating wildly and his breaths were rapid and shallow.

This was not the first time this had happened, he remembered. A few months after his release, he had been invited to join a group of local pastors for lunch. At one point, one of them had asked him how he planned to spend his spare time, now that he had his freedom. In a flash of insight, he knew he had no answer for them, at least not an answer that they could understand, with their evenings of television and summer vacations at the beach and hours spent in church planning meetings and church development meetings and building committee meetings. With his heart pounding, he snatched enough air to gasp out, "I don't know yet." He managed a half-smile and held out his sweaty hands, palms up. After a second or two, the conversation started up again, and within a few minutes, he was himself again. But the experience had frightened and disturbed him. Now, the episodes had started up again and were occurring with increasing frequency.

Lord, I don't know why I'm feeling this way, but please, help me calm down. Help me to understand what's happening. James forced himself to take several deep breaths. The agitation began to subside. He turned the key in the ignition and put the truck in reverse.

Most afternoons he returned to the boarding house a half hour or so before supper, cheerful and friendly, speaking to all the other guests, asking about their day. Today, he smiled absentmindedly at anyone who spoke to him, and proceeded directly to his bedroom. It was not his habit to lie on the bed during the day, not unless he was sick, but today he climbed in and pulled a crocheted afghan over him, though it was quite warm upstairs.

His mind meandered back over the last thirty years, stopping here and there to fill in scenes of the story. His story. How much of his story was left to live? His life was, in all probability, two-thirds over, and what did his memories consist of? Lots of dingy gray walls and hours of reading and praying and keeping himself busy to keep from dwelling on his circumstances.

He was grateful for the last two years, he truly was, and thrilled to be a free man again, to spend time with his son and daughter-in-law, to anticipate the imminent arrival of a grandchild. Still, disappointment was heavy for the life that could have been, if he hadn't been locked away most of his life. And though it was through no fault of his, he felt a deep shame that he had not been there to support his wife through her years of illness and suffering. That was a husband's duty, after all. Nor had he been there for his son, to fulfill a father's duty. Over all, he thought, his life didn't compare very favorably to those of most men his age. The feelings overwhelmed him, and he began to pray, lifting up all those thoughts and concerns, stopping only when sleep overtook him.

Fourteen

Alone in the back yard, Ethan was slowly swinging on the bench swing he had hung from the largest branch of the hickory tree. It was a good place to think. Right now, he was feeling bewildered by the heated discussion he had just had with his wife. Of course, he realized she was not quite her normal, logical, reasonable self, being eight months pregnant in the heat of summer. Still, how could they have both been so unaware of the other's position on this matter? If he were a betting man, he would have been willing to risk his money on the question of whether or not they had already agreed that Grace would not be working once they had started their family. Evidently, they had not already agreed.

Today, Grace was adamant that she would continue working part-time for the newspaper. She said she already had everything worked out with Joe Wilson, the editor. Ethan didn't like it, not one bit. How would that make him look as a pastor, if all his flock saw his wife leaving their children to go to work every day? She needed to be at home, available for their offspring and for him. Not that he wasn't proud of her accomplishments and her intelligence, but he believed that the breadwinning role should be his and his alone. Working before the baby came was entirely different. It was temporary and purely voluntary.

His own mother had never worked outside the home. Well, sure, she substituted at the elementary school occasionally. *Occasionally*, so that it never interfered with their home life. And, on the side, she did do a small amount of sewing for she was an excellent seamstress. But that was all. Basically, she was a homemaker. Grace ought to be able to understand the importance of making a home for their children.

Besides that, if he took the job with Harry Carroll, there really would be no other viable choice. Grace would have to stay home, because he would be out of town so much. He hadn't actually reached a decision yet about accepting the position, but he didn't want the issue of Grace's work to have any bearing on the situation.

He sighed. Maybe Dad or Clare could talk some sense into his wife.

Fifteen

"I'm fine, Joe!" Grace gave her boss her most sincere, most serious look. "I'm not due for another three weeks, and I feel great," she insisted, as she lowered herself carefully into her swivel chair.

"I'm sure you do, but you remember Ed said he wouldn't mind a bit coming over and filling in next week?" Joe's concern showed on his face. "Both of our kids were born two weeks before the due date, and Marjorie swears it was because she kept working full-time right up until the very day." He watched for some relenting on her part. Seeing none, he dropped his head in resignation. "You know everyone in town, including your husband, will blame me for forcing you to work if you deliver next week."

A peek at Grace told him he had gone too far. He put his hands up in mock protection as she erupted. "For the last time, Joe: I…am.…fine. Now. You and your family go on to Myrtle Beach for your vacation and stop irritating me about this!"

Joe was already backing up into his office. "Okay, okay," he said in a placating tone. "Just promise me you'll call Ed if you start feeling the least bit tired." Without waiting for a reply, he eased through the door, closing it quickly behind him.

Grace grabbed a copy of last week's paper, folded it once, and began fanning. Gee whiz, it was hot today. And what was the matter with everybody? You'd think she had a terminal disease, instead of just being pregnant. Did they think that just because she was expecting she couldn't do her job anymore? It was perfectly clear that her normally reasonable husband felt that way, based on his over-protective comments over breakfast at home this morning.

And then, as it frequently did lately, her perspective totally flip-flopped, and instead of asking what was wrong with everybody else, she was asking what was the matter with herself today? She couldn't believe how rude she had just been to Joe. And earlier this morning, that scene with Ethan, who was arguably the sweetest, kindest man in the world. He had said almost the same thing as Joe, and she had yelled at him! She never yelled at Ethan. Uh-oh. She could feel the tears welling up. Holding her back with her right hand and her makeup bag with the left, she waddled quickly to the restroom to have a little cry in private.

Sixteen

The next thing James heard was Clare, knocking softly on his door. "James, supper's ready. Are you coming down?"

His first thought was, what a comforting voice she had. His second thought was relief. Whatever had had him in its grip had been banished and he was starving. "Yes, I'm coming." Throwing off the afghan, he bounded out of bed and threw open the door, beaming at his friend. "What's for supper tonight?"

They practically skipped down the stairs together, conversing busily, as if they were old friends who hadn't seen each other in a long, long time.

"Here, James, I'll do that. Give me those dishes." Clare held out her hands, but James went on clearing the table, purposely ignoring her. "Aren't you going to work on your house this evening?"

"I don't know. Maybe. Maybe not."

That uncharacteristic indecision brought a bemused expression to Clare's face. "Well, don't worry about this mess. I've got it covered. Go do something you want to do."

He considered that suggestion but he couldn't think of anything he wanted to do or anywhere he wanted to go. He felt pretty comfortable right here with Clare, and after the attack of anxiety earlier that day, comfort felt... well, very comforting. "I think I'll just hang around here this evening," he said thoughtfully. He remembered Sophie's birthday. "Hey, maybe you could help me with something."

"Sure. What do you need?"

"Well," he laughed in embarrassment. "Bo Lucas asked me to pick out a birthday present for Sophie. You know. His little girl? Five years old?"

"Yes, I know Sophie's mother, Katrina. Sophie's a sweet kid. And you're supposed to get the present, huh?"

"Yep. And I don't know anything about what a little girl would like nowadays. I might have been able to take a good guess at it – fifty years ago! But now? I don't know where to start."

"I'm sure we can find something. In fact, it's Friday night, so most of the stores are open until nine. We could put the dishes in to soak, and go right now. Want to?"

Throwing a look of pure gratitude her way, he grabbed a stack of dishes and headed for the kitchen.

All the way downtown, Clare kept up a cheerful banter, trying to engage James in the conversation but with little success. She had hoped for more. He actually seemed nervous, she thought, though that idea was ridiculous since he had been a minister, one way or another, for thirty five years and was used to talking to groups and individuals about all manner of difficult subjects. So, he couldn't possibly be uneasy conversing with someone he saw every single day. She remembered what Grace had said a few days earlier. Maybe she should follow her friend's advice and simply tell James how she felt.

When they reached the town's small department store, he came around and opened the door of the truck for her. He offered his hand, and she took it, rewarding him with a warm smile of thanks. The smile and the eye contact seemed to unnerve him, for he dropped her hand

and turned to face the store. Disappointed again, she shook it off and led the way into the store.

"The toy department is this way," she motioned. Going straight to the aisle of dolls, she stopped in front of the Barbie section. "A five year old is definitely old enough to enjoy a Barbie doll," said Clare. "How much money do we have?"

"Twenty-five dollars. Will that be enough? Because I could put some more money with that…"

"That's a gracious plenty." She perused the shelves, and chose several items. "Let's start with this one. She's wearing a nice party dress and shoes, plus she comes with an extra outfit. That's ten dollars. Then, we can get a Ken doll, too." She looked to James for approval. "How does that sound?"

"Sounds terrific to me. Is that what five year olds like?"

"Oh, yeah. Big time." Clare went back to the racks. "Ooooh, look! These are on sale!" She couldn't help herself, she was actually giggling, she was so pleased with herself. "Here's a carrying case, to hold the dolls and their clothes and accessories! She'll love this, James." Without thinking, Clare grabbed his arm and hugged it against her. When she realized he was standing stiffly, she quickly released him.

"That ought to do it," she said brightly, to hide her embarrassment. She glanced toward the front of the store. "Ready to check out?"

Within a few minutes they were all done and James was backing the truck out of the parking space. Clare was feeling a little irritated with the way his attitude seemed to swing from one extreme to the other. Earlier at the boarding house, before, during and after supper, he was charmingly friendly and open, then, just minutes later, riding over here in the truck and during shopping, he acted distant and uncomfortable. She couldn't figure it out, so she decided to take the plunge. "James, I need to talk to you about something," she said quickly, before she could change her mind.

"Sure. What is it?" They were pulling into her driveway now.

"Just turn off the truck and let's sit here a minute," she said.

"All right." He did as she asked but kept looking straight ahead.

"James, we've known each other for two years now, and we've become good friends, don't you think?"

"Yes." He looked at her questioningly. "Yes, we have."

"Well...," she hesitated, her resolve wavering.

"Clare, is something wrong?"

"No," she reassured him, "there's nothing wrong, it's just..." She took a deep breath and continued, looking down at her hands. "For quite a while now, I've been aware of a change in the way I feel about you. That is, I feel more than just friendship. I haven't wanted to rush you because I know you've had a lot to deal with in the last two years, but James, I'd like to be more than just your friend. Sometimes, you give me the impression that you feel something for me, too. But, other times, like tonight at the store, I think maybe I've imagined it." She stopped and waited for a response. There was none. She grew more and more embarrassed as the seconds ticked by.

"I'm sorry," she murmured. "Guess I shouldn't have said anything." Slipping out of the truck, Clare ran to the back door and whisked inside.

Seventeen

Still as death, James sat unmoving in the truck. The only thing breaking through the numbness was the constriction building in his chest. Going inside was not an option, for to see Clare again tonight would shatter his meager control. Better to take a drive, he thought. Clear his head.

As he backed out of the drive, his first thought was to visit Ethan for some encouragement and Godly counsel, but then he remembered. If today's disagreement between the young couple was any indication, Ethan had quite a bit to deal with himself these days. So for now, he would not burden his son with any of his vague emotional and physical symptoms.

He drove up and down the residential streets of the small town, finally coming to rest at the town square. The streetlamps' glow was inviting and the night was pleasantly warm, so he got out of the truck and sat on one of the many benches scattered across the courthouse lawn.

It wasn't long before the peace of the night began to soothe his agitated spirit. Relaxing, he stretched his legs out, crossed his arms and leaned his head back against the bench. The slight breeze high in the old oaks was rustling the dry leaves, loosening a few here and there, to dance gently to the earth. He felt a moment of pure gratitude and joy, to be able to sit outside on such a night, to feel and see such a simple, beautiful moment. He would never take such moments for granted, he thought. Not after missing so many of them.

He was thus in his thoughts and did not see the dark shadow of a man approach from across the street.

"James?"

Startled, James sat up quickly.

"Didn't mean to startle you, dear friend," the tall stately gentleman assured him. "If you'd rather be alone with your thoughts this evening, we can postpone this visit until a later date."

"Martin!" James stood to shake his friend's hand. "Not at all. I always welcome the chance to have a good talk with you." He nodded toward the bench. "Would you rather sit," then he swept his arm toward the sidewalk, "or walk?"

Martin Sawyer chuckled and leaned his head in to share a confidence. "I'd really like to go back in the house to my easy chair and share a glass of my special homemade wine. What say you?"

"I say, it's been a long time since I've tasted any of your homemade wine. Lead on!"

While Martin poured the wine, James studied the photos and other mementos placed tastefully throughout the study. It probably hadn't occurred to Martin, but James realized that the last time he had visited his friend, Martin and his wife still lived in the large Victorian home several blocks away. This new living arrangement, with Martin's living quarters above his ground floor law offices, had existed for more than ten years, ever since the death of Martin's wife.

I haven't visited Martin in his home in thirty years, he thought. He'd missed thirty years of life on the outside. Sometimes it felt like he was so far behind everyone else that there was no hope of ever catching up. Though his mind and spirit told him otherwise, his emotions remained confused and despondent.

"James?"

Martin's arm was extended, offering the scuppernong wine, and his look was one of gentle concern. With a flash of insight, James realized he must have been unresponsive for a moment or two, lost in his thoughts.

Slightly embarrassed, James took the glass. "Thanks," he murmured.

"Come and sit." Martin gestured toward the hearth, where a low fire burned and two particularly comfortable-looking chairs waited on each side. "As my years have advanced, James, the distance between me and the fire has decreased proportionately, so if it gets too toasty for you, just slide your chair back a bit."

"Do I recognize Jed Liles' workmanship on these chairs?"

"Yes, indeed." Martin crossed his leg and leaned back in his chair. "In fact, I have several more pieces of his scattered throughout the house. The man is a genius in his field."

"He certainly is," James agreed. An easy silence ensued as they stared at the fire.

"Do you like the wine?" Martin asked.

"It's luscious, almost like eating a scuppernong. Just as I remembered it from so long ago."

"Many years have gone by, haven't they, James?"

James nodded.

"James, I have wondered – the few times I've seen you since your release – if your adjustment to your new life has been….difficult?" James was staring at the fire, not answering. Martin continued. "It is far from my intent to delve into your private thoughts, but since our first meeting - back when we were young and strong and dreaming young men's dreams – we have shared a friendship of the highest order, which has always been most precious to me. I suppose what I am trying to express, and handling rather poorly, is that I am available, as your friend, should you ever need to talk things over with someone."

As James listened to Martin speak, he understood that their meeting tonight was no coincidence. As it had always been throughout his life, God was providing what he needed, at the precise moment of his need.

Overcome, James put his head in his hands and thanked his Father, his eyes growing moist.

Then, lifting his head, he wiped his eyes and smiled at his old friend. "I do need to talk."

"As you wish, my friend."

James took a deep breath and exhaled slowly through his mouth. "I don't know where to begin, Martin." He thought a moment. "I've had several episodes of…I don't know…something resembling sheer panic. My heart pounds, I can't breathe, I can't think or move. And it's never over anything deserving such anxiety."

"You weren't in a stressful situation at those times?"

"Not really. The first time was at the pastors' dinner a few months after my release. It was such a sincere gesture of welcome, a kindness that I greatly appreciated. But someone asked me a question, about what I planned to do with the rest of my life, and I completely choked. I was barely able to reply."

"And the other times?"

"Sometimes I wake in the night, usually after I've dreamed of Betty. I dream I've lost her in the darkness, in the mountain's night mist, and I can't get to her, no matter how hard I try. When I wake my heart aches for her and this great feeling of loss washes over me. Plus the same heart pounding and inability to breathe."

"This happens a lot?"

"Two or three times a week." James shrugged. "And a few other times, when I've been asked a question, or I have an obligation to perform, I become so overwhelmed with the demand, even though it's nothing big or important, that I have a totally unwarranted reaction. I become so anxious I can't function at all. For a while anyway."

James stopped talking and the room was silent, save for the crackle and "shhh" of the fire.

Martin tapped his finger alongside his nose. "I think I know someone you should talk to."

Eighteen

Sunday
August 23

It was a nice, lazy Sunday afternoon. Grace was stretched out on the couch with her feet propped up in Ethan's lap. She was reading the newspaper and he was studying the materials from Harry Carroll's organization. Putting the folder down, he picked up her foot and began rubbing. Should he disturb this moment of peace? He desperately wanted to talk over the pros and cons of joining the evangelist's team. Grace had a great head for dissecting a problem and figuring out what was really important.

When he switched to the other foot, she dropped the newspaper a few inches to peer at him over the top. "That feels wonderful, sweetheart. My feet almost feel normal again."

"You know, your feet probably wouldn't swell so much if you'd stay off your feet."

"I know, but I can't just sit here – or stay in the bed – all day long. You know it would drive me crazy!"

He was about to say that she could at least cut back a bit, but then he thought better of it. Her emotions were running close to the surface and she had been very defensive lately about him telling her what to do. Very out of character for his normally imperturbable spouse, but evidently not unusual during pregnancy, as he had been told frequently by just about everyone in town.

"Oh!" Grace started. Quickly she took Ethan's hand and placed it on her stomach, never taking her eyes off of his. They were both grinning at the forceful thumping taking place just underneath her skin. "This is one of the reasons I wake up in the middle of the night!" she giggled.

Gently he slid his hand across, trying to feel all the nuances of their baby's movements. "Amazing. How did God think to do this?"

"I can't wait to see him. Or her," she said. "I don't care one whit which. Do you? Truthfully now."

He shook his head. "I only want you and the baby to be healthy." Stretching up toward her head, being careful not to put his weight on her, Ethan leaned in and kissed her, then whispered, "I love you so much."

She graced him with a lop-sided smile. "I love you, too, Skidroe." Then she raised her eyebrows a little, and he knew she was about to ask for something. "Would you rub my legs, too? That felt so good."

"Yes, ma'am," he acquiesced. He would rub her legs all day if she would just talk to him about some of these issues. For several minutes he massaged her legs, until he could tell that she was feeling relaxed, then he broached a difficult subject.

"Sweet Grace?"

"Mmm-hmmm." Her voice was slightly muffled for she had let the newspaper fall over her face.

"We need to talk about Harry Carroll's offer."

Ethan could feel a slight change in the muscle tension in her legs. "Yes? What about it?" she said, through the sheets of newsprint.

He hadn't planned on speaking to the back page of the newspaper. "Well, they gave me a month to think about it and we've still got plenty of time to make a final decision, but I'd really like to know what you think about the whole idea."

Silence from the pages of The Fairmount Chronicle.

"Grace?"

She flipped the pages away and her tone was snippy as she replied, "Ethan? Very soon I'm going to have a baby. And that baby needs a father." Her lips trembled. "And I need you to be here, too."

Ethan gathered her up and pulled her into his lap. What should he say? She wasn't actually discussing the issue at hand, she was just getting emotional. How could he tell if this was the hormones talking, or if she meant that he shouldn't take the job? He decided to take the easiest way out.

"Okay, honey, okay. You know I'll always be here for you."

"I know you will, sweetheart." She snuggled even closer. "Did I tell you I talked to Mom yesterday?"

"No. What did she say?"

"She said she would be here a week from Tuesday. Oh, and she said not to worry about cleaning out your office here. She said she would rather stay with Clare."

"Oh. Well… now I feel like a chump because I haven't already cleaned it out. With the guest bedroom becoming the nursery, I knew we'd need to get rid of the office, or at least clear it out some, so we could put the double bed in there." Ethan was clearly irritated with himself. "Can't you call her back and ask her to stay here instead?"

"Well, I could. You know I love my mother, but she's planning on staying several weeks, and sometimes we clash a little if we're together too much, so…."

Ethan waited for her to finish.

"Let's leave it the way it is. Besides, you know how close she's gotten to Clare. They're like two teeny-boppers, dancing around and singing "their" songs, talking about old movies… She'll be here with me a lot, helping with the baby, but this way she'll have some time to herself. And so will we."

Ethan nodded in agreement, all the while wondering why it was that she could be so reasonable and logical and willing to talk about some things, and yet so totally unhinged when he wanted to talk about their future.

Hormones!

Nineteen

Monday
August 24

The first day that Joe was on vacation, Grace was a little late getting to work. A good night's sleep was getting harder and harder to get, though she had tried every position imaginable to accommodate her now enormous belly. At three a.m. she had finally moved to the sofa, taking with her three pillows for support, and was able to snooze off and on for the rest of the night. Still, it wasn't enough and when she woke, she was feeling a little "ill", in the Southern sense of the word.

Of course, Ethan was his usual thoughtful self. Fixed breakfast for her. Helped her get her shoes tied, because her Keds were the only shoes that were comfortable anymore and she could just barely touch her feet, much less hang around down there long enough to tie a bow. The whole Keds thing was getting old, too. One of Grace's trademarks was her sense of style and there were only so many looks she could create that included Keds. Especially when she could only shop in the maternity department.

At any rate, she was at the office now and was ready to take full responsibility for managing the newspaper for the next two weeks. She made a point of stopping by every employee's desk – there were only five, so it didn't take long – to make sure they were all on board with this week's assignments.

Jacalyn Wilson

She was just getting settled at her desk when the front desk receptionist buzzed her. "Grace, it's Joe on line two." Grace could feel a little fuming coming on, as she was thinking, *Good grief, does he think I'm so incompetent that he's got to call and check on me first thing Monday morning?* Wisdom and caution prevailed however, and her cool but professional greeting was, "Good morning, Joe. How's the weather at the beach?"

"Oh, it's great and we're having a super time. How's everything at the office?"

Curtly, she replied, "Everything's fine, Joe."

"Oh, I knew it would be. Listen, the reason I'm calling has to do with the Stockton Corporation. Have you interviewed the rep yet?"

Ruffled feathers soothed and her interest piqued, Clare answered, "Well, no. I was planning to contact him today and set up an interview. Why? What's going on?"

"After you talk to him, go ahead and write your article, but stay away from any sort of implied approval of the project. Stick to what the gentleman tells you and nothing else."

"What in the world is going on, Joe?"

"I met up with a college buddy of mine. His family is staying in the condos next to ours. Fancy, shmancy place, too. Anyway, this guy is an investment guru in New York, keeps up with everything going on in the corporate world. I just happened to mention that Heaven's Mountain might soon be home to a world class resort. He wanted to know all about it. As soon as I mentioned the Stockton Corporation, he started shaking his head. He's familiar with the company. Says the Stockton Corporation is a subsidiary of a larger corporation, Stockton Development and Acquisitions. He says their specialty is buying huge tracts of undeveloped land that have some hidden natural resource. Then they find a buyer, or maybe they already have a buyer, who harvests that resource and sells it."

"But the gold has already been mined. There's nothing else up there. Timber?"

"Not unless they have come up with some way to navigate all that heavy equipment in and out of all those hollows. Besides, there's plenty of timber at lower elevations, so why bother?"

"Yeah, it doesn't make sense. Okay, so what do you want me to do?"

"Right now, I only want you to talk to Mr. English. See what he has to say, but don't mention what I've told you. Just pay close attention and try to determine if he's telling the truth, at least as he knows it."

"Okay, I'll do that today, if possible."

"Good. I also want you to check the county office for any new permits filed by the Stockton Corporation, or any company whose name you don't recognize. Especially any mining or harvesting of any kind of assets."

"Will do."

"My buddy is going to have someone in his office take a look at what Stockton is up to, also. Do you know if any property owners have signed options yet?"

"Not that I'm aware of."

"Well, you'd better check that, too. If this is true, I hope we can get the word out before anyone lets their property go."

"Me, too."

"Well, Grace, I feel a little guilty dumping all this on you but....I've got to go now. Jack is waiting for me at the beach."

"Oh, ha-ha! I can hear the regret in your voice, Boss. You guys have a wonderful vacation and don't spend too much time working on this."

When she hung up, Grace had to admit she felt an uncharacteristic tiredness, just thinking about all the extra work that had fallen into her lap. Must be all that sleep she had been missing. Or all this extra weight...

Twenty

Thelma was feeling her age as she cracked a half dozen eggs to scramble. Billy had gotten in late last night after a week at baseball camp and her great-niece was visiting, too, so that old arthritis pain in her joints would just have to be ignored while she prepared a proper breakfast for the young folks. Homemade biscuits were in the oven and the thick-sliced sugar-cured bacon was sitting to the side, perfectly browned and crispy.

Who'd have ever thought that she, plain and simple Thelma Canfield, would be cooking breakfast in this fine kitchen, not as a servant but as mistress of the house? She had certainly never imagined it, and it still felt strange to her, even after more than two years. When Preacher James was pardoned, a number of interesting details had come to light, one of which was the fact that Thelma's brother, Amos Canfield, had never signed over the Canfield homeplace property to Beamon Lucas as payment for a gambling debt. The truth was that Beamon Lucas, who was Billy's grandfather, had forged the document then coerced his son Bo Lucas, Billy's father, to kill Amos, with the full knowledge that the gold vein running through that mountainside would make him a very rich man. With the gold in hand and no moral scruples holding him back, Beamon had built an empire that controlled the whole county and then some.

Thelma never asked for restitution, never even had a hankering for all that money and the extra worries it would bring. What would she want with this big house and all that money and property? The courts, at Bo and Billy's request, had come up with an equitable division of the assets, with all the Canfield property restored to Thelma, plus a considerable portion of everything else, including this house, formerly the home of Beamon and Sadie Lucas. Though Bo Lucas retained ownership of numerous rental properties and various businesses in town, Thelma had insisted that Billy remain with her in the only home he had ever known and he was only too happy to comply. With his father in prison and both of his grandparents dead, Billy found the presence of their former housekeeper to be a secure, comfortable relationship.

"Mornin', Thelma," mumbled Billy as he stumbled by, rubbing his eyes.

"Good mornin', boy. D'ju sleep good?"

"Yes, ma'am," he answered. He stopped and put his arm around her shoulders as he snitched a piece of bacon. "Is this all we're having?" he asked with all seriousness.

She raised one eyebrow. "You need to just go on, now. I can see you've got your smarty britches on this morning." She slapped playfully at his hand as he snuck another piece of bacon. "And get out of that bacon. Katherine's here for a few weeks, and she and I might want a little, too."

"Kate's here? Why didn't you tell me?" Bacon forgotten, he sprinted for the stairs. "I'm gonna go wake her up!"

Before Thelma could say "don't" he was halfway up. Those two! They were always getting into something, cooking up mischief usually, but nothing too dastardly, thank goodness. In Thelma's opinion, childless and inexperienced as she was, they were good for each other. Billy had been knocked out of his usual orbit when both his grandparents died and his father went to jail, and little Katherine had always had to fend for herself, with a mama who stayed drunk most of the time and a daddy too busy to notice her.

It didn't take long for Billy to take care of business. Stomping, pouty, and bleary-eyed, Katherine entered the kitchen. "Oh, good golly Pete, Aunt Thelma," she whined. "Why'd you let him wake me up? I wanted to sleep late this morning!"

Billy stood over to the side, grinning and not one bit sorry.

"Good morning, Katherine. No use crying over spilt milk." Thelma looked at Billy. "Besides, now you've got all day to figure out how you're going to get back at him. Sit down and eat. You, too, Billy."

They sat, one on each side of Thelma, and she took their hands and said the blessing. As soon as she finished, Billy jumped up, grabbed a mug from the cabinet and proceeded to pour himself a cup of coffee as Thelma and Katherine exchanged skeptical glances. Not to be outdone, Katherine immediately followed suit, pouring herself a cup, too.

Thelma huffed, "Now, if you're all finished with this silliness – and both of you too young to be drinking coffee - set yourselves down and eat. And I hope you know that coffee will stunt your growth."

Billy at six-two and Katherine at five-eight exchanged an amused glance. "I think it's too late for that, Aunt Thelma," she said.

"I know that, child," said Thelma, gracing them with one of her rare smiles. "I was just picking at you." Lord, she loved these two scalawags.

Twenty-One

"As far as I know, Mr. English has not approached my father yet, Miss Sally. Dad and Mr. English are both staying at Miss Clare's boarding house, but I guess he just hasn't realized that Dad is one of the property owners. Of course, Mr. English has only been here a few days," Ethan commented.

The octogenarian's voice was warbly with age. "Well, he come up here t'see me yestiddy. Hit was a lot of money, but I jest don't see myself livin' anywhar 'cept hyere."

Ethan sympathized, "I'm sure it's a difficult decision."

Miss Sally warmed to the subject. "My granddaddy owned land in this holler, and that's how I come by it. I allus figgered I'd be laid out for my wake ri'chere in the front room."

Miss Sally was a lifelong member of Heaven's Mountain Church, and Ethan knew his father would want to visit her, to give her what assurance he could. "Would you like me to tell Dad to come talk to you about it?" he asked kindly.

"Yes-sir, Rev'rend, I'd 'preciate if you would do that for me." Done with the first subject, she switched horses in mid-stream. "Now when's your first young'un s'posed to get here, Preacher?"

"Should be about three and a half more weeks," he said.

"No-sir, there'll be a full moon in ten days. I s'pect that child will be comin' about then. Hit'll be sooner than three weeks."

"Well, you may be right about that," said Ethan, humoring her. "I guess we'll just have to wait and see."

Later, when Ethan came out of his office, Mrs. Pons was typing away on Sunday's bulletin. She stopped to hold out a stack of stamped letters. "If you're going near the post office," she asked, "would you mind taking these?"

"Sure. Do we need stamps today?"

"No. We're good for a while yet." She hesitated. "One other thing, though, and I kind of hate to even mention this..." she said diffidently. "But you know Grace has put on, well, I hate to say it, but maybe a little more weight than she should have, plus she's got that dark, whiskey-colored hair. It just reminds me of my cousin Velma. She was just the same, and..."

Ethan's expression turned stony as he tried to listen and pray for patience at the same time.

"...there's no other way to say it, she just went slightly crazy after the baby came. She was never the same. But you will just watch for that, won't you, Preacher? After the baby comes?"

"Yes. Yes, ma'am," he said to the well-meaning matronly woman behind the desk, while he backed toward the door. "Yes, I surely will," he said as he went out and shut the door firmly behind him.

"Heavens to Mergatroid!" he exclaimed under his breath as he cranked up the car. "Does everyone in town have something they've just got to share with me about having a baby?"

Twenty-Two

"Excuse me."

Clare nearly jumped out of the dining room chair, so deep in thought was she. The embarrassing scene with James a few days ago had been running through her head, over and over, as she attempted to uncover any missteps on her part. The only possible conclusion was that James had no romantic interest in her.

And now here was another boarder, the handsome Mr. English, no less, disturbing this rare moment of post-breakfast quiet. He probably needed some towels or something even more mundane from her. After all, she was simply a glorified maid if you got right down to it. Not that there was anything wrong with being a maid…

"I'm sorry I startled you. Come to think of it, this is the first time I've seen you sitting down or taking a break of any kind, so I'm doubly sorry to interrupt. Shall I come back later?"

Clare waved her hand, dismissing the importance of the disruption. Standing, she began scraping and stacking the breakfast dishes. Intent on her task and without looking at him, she tried and failed to keep her voice from sounding brittle as she asked, "What do you need, Mr. English? Do you need more towels? Is everything all right with your room?"

"Oh, everything is wonderful," he assured her. "I couldn't ask for better accommodations or service – or food! You are an excellent cook, Clare."

Ashamed of her cool attitude, and overwhelmed by the generous compliments, she stopped her stacking to give him a grateful smile. "Thank you very much, sir." Her smile changed to a sheepish grin. "I admit that I needed a kind word this morning, so thank you. But what was it you needed?"

"Oh. Well." He rubbed his hands together in anticipation. "I was hoping you might be able to spare a little time today. I'd like to meet the artisan who creates those incredible armchairs. Could we go today?"

Clare put her hand on her hip and cocked her head, thinking. She actually had a number of chores planned for the day. But, on the other hand, here was this lovely handsome man standing in front of her and… Oh, what the heck! James was obviously never going to make a move so she might as well explore other options. There was nothing on her chore list that couldn't wait until another day.

She gave him her answer. "We certainly can. How about right after lunch, Mr. English?"

"Perfect! And why don't you call me Tom?"

"Tom it is, then. And you may call me Clare."

"Take the next right, Tom. Just past the Pure oil sign."

"Right here?"

"Yes, this is it," she said, as he made a smooth tight turn in the sporty (red, of course) Camaro. Clare was feeling very glad indeed that she was on this little jaunt with her new friend. This was in spite of the fact that she was losing a whole day of work, rather than half a day. She had spent most of the morning fixing her hair in a sleek pageboy, taking extra time with her makeup, and trying on outfits, settling on a nautical style suit, navy, white and bright yellow. (She liked it because it reminded her of something Jackie Kennedy might wear.) She rarely wore anything other than her work Levi's and simple cotton shirts, except for her Sunday dresses of course, so wearing something casual, but fun and stylish, made her feel as if she actually had a life. Of course, the bluster of the wind in the open convertible had made short work of her neat hairdo, but she found some comfort in the fact that he had seen her before her hair was blown to smithereens. In fact, when she came down the stairs in the boarding house, the look he gave her was one of genuine admiration, so she could live with the tousled look, she thought.

Though it had only been ten minutes since they left the house, already Clare was relaxed and comfortable with Tom English. It was so easy to talk to him, and it didn't hurt anything that he was exceedingly generous with his compliments. She had no illusions that she was anything but a plain old hardworking mountain girl with no more than a basic education, and yet this man, a widely traveled, intelligent, successful man of the world, was treating her as if she was a rare treasure to be greatly admired.

A girl could get used to this.

Fifteen minutes later they were pulling into the parking lot of a long, tin-roofed shop displaying the sign "Liles Fine Furniture". Jed Liles seemed quite happy to open up his workshop and take them on a tour, displaying his work in various stages of completion. He had only three completed pieces in the shop. "They go out just about as fast as I can finish them," he admitted. "These two – the sofa and matching chair – are already sold. This chair here, well, my wife liked this fabric, so I made it up for her. 'Course if a buyer comes along and wants it, she'll let it go." He laughed. "Happens all the time. Her choice, not mine!"

Tom inquired, "Would you mind if I took some pictures?"

"Go right ahead," answered Jed.

With his Polaroid instant camera, Tom took a number of pictures to send to his sister. Most of the photos included Clare, somewhat reluctant to pose but smiling nonetheless. She stomped her foot in mock aggravation when asked to pose outside for a shot of the shop itself. "No! You get in this one. I'll take the picture." She bustled over and removed the camera from his hands. "Now, stand right there under the sign, and make sure I'm getting your good side, Tom," she teased, while admitting to herself that the man did not have a bad side.

Afterwards, as they were walking back to the car, he asked, "By any chance, do you have enough time to drive up to the top of the mountain? I hear there's a magnificent view from a lookout point, but they say it's rather difficult to find the turnoff."

"Oh, that's true. You have to go down one of the old mining roads to get to the view." It took Clare about a half second to decide she simply could not take the rest of the afternoon off. "I wish I could," she said with obvious disappointment. "But all those pesky boarders expect something to eat this evening," she joked. When Tom opened her door, she slid in with the ease of a teenager and graced him with a flirty smile. "Just let me know if you'd like to go another day, and I'll make the arrangements ahead of time."

He was certainly comfortable to be with, she thought, studying the handsome figure he cut coming around the front of the car. They'd only spent a few hours together, and already their conversation was easy and flowing. Then a picture of James popped into her mind, and she thrust it aside, still a little hurt and confused by his recent behavior. She wasn't going to mope around and wait forever, not even for James. This little outing with Tom was doing wonders for her self-confidence, and she wasn't going to waste one minute of it pining away for something that could never be.

"Have you always lived here?" he asked.

"I've lived here for the last seven years. Ever since my aunt passed away and left me the boarding house." She looked his way. "But I've always been a mountain girl. All my folks still live not much more than an hour's drive away." As she remembered, her voice took on a far-away tone. "Things were different when I was little, especially way up in the mountains, back in some of the real remote hollers and ridges. Some of those folks didn't see anybody but their own kin for months on end. You could see it in their eyes sometimes, too, almost like they were lost when they came to town, amongst all of us." She paused, and when she spoke again, there was pride in her voice. "But you'd be surprised at the talent and gifts they cultivated, up there in the backwoods. The women could hand-sew a quilt fine enough for a queen. And the men's fingers could fly when they played the fiddle or the mandolin."

"You make me want to see the quilts and hear the fiddles, Clare," he said, with sincere interest. "Tell me more about growing up in the mountains."

He managed to get her going, though she needed little urging. During the fifteen minute ride, their laughter rippled and bounced around the small car as she shared story after story of childhood escapades. As they were pulling into the driveway of the boarding house, she had just gotten to the good part of the pet mouse story, where the mouse was crawling out of her daddy's overall pocket during the preacher's sermon one Sunday morning, so of course, they had to stay in the car until the story concluded. When he came around to open her car door, they were both still smiling and laughing so it seemed most natural for Tom to put his arm loosely around her shoulder as they walked companionably to the back steps.

Clare didn't notice James standing at his bedroom window gazing down at the two of them.

Twenty-Three

I'm so smart, thought Clare. She was congratulating herself on having the foresight to take two chicken casseroles out of the freezer – the ones she kept "made ahead" for funerals and such - before she left on her outing with Mr. English. Or rather, with Tom. After leaving him at the foot of the staircase, she hit the kitchen running, flipping the oven temperature to 350 degrees, throwing the casseroles in, and running into her bedroom to change into her jeans.

Back in the kitchen, she started in on the vegetables. Tonight's bread would just have to be "wop" biscuits, those canned refrigerated wonders that you could "wop" up against the corner of the counter to pop the can open.

For a brief moment she wondered what was keeping James. He frequently came to the kitchen and helped her with meal preparation. No matter. It was probably best that they keep their distance for a few days, until the memory of their strange evening had time to fade a little.

She began peeling potatoes, thinking about this morning at breakfast. They had both been polite but aloof. She might have imagined it, but a couple of times she had gotten the impression he wanted to say something to her. Tuff stuff. He ought to suffer just a little. He should have at least responded with *something* after she bared her soul to him like that. Instead, he sat there like a knot on a log. Yes, she thought, he deserved to be uncomfortable for a while.

Clare was placing the last of the serving bowls on the long dining room table, when she noticed that Tom had moved from his usual seat and had situated himself in the chair to her right. James was already in his customary place on her left. This should be interesting, she thought. Nevertheless, she was determined to enjoy Tom's company at dinner. And she did.

James was mostly quiet, offering only a few words now and then, and though he did not stare or appear to be eavesdropping on the animated conversation between Tom and herself, she somehow knew that he was taking in every word and every look. He was the first to leave the dinner table, another tell-tale sign of his poorly masked feelings. Though she didn't miss a beat in her spirited debate with Tom, she noticed when James left by the back door.

The rest of the evening Clare spent in the front parlor, talking to Tom about all the places he'd been. Europe, Japan, Brazil, and all over the States. Still, as pleasant as the attention was to her, there was a bothersome little window flapping deep in her heart, keeping something in or letting something out. She didn't know which.

Twenty-Four

James was driving. Thinking. Praying. Without making a conscious decision he wound up at the little white church near the top of Heaven's Mountain. His feet carried him through the grass, wet with dew now, to the small cemetery beside the church. He wanted the comfort of being with his wife tonight.

Usually, when he visited Betty's grave, he felt a closeness with her. Oh, he knew she was with Jesus, so perhaps what he felt was just his own memories come to life. Still, he had lost so much of his married life, he greedily grasped even the feeling of being with her.

Ignoring the dampness of the ground, he sat down, leaning back against the gravestone, but his distress was not eased. Though he waited for the relief to come, there was no soothing of his tension or his turmoil. Tonight was different, for thoughts of Clare kept slipping in and out of his consciousness.

Finally the chill of his wet clothing penetrated deeply enough to get his attention and he rose stiffly. The side door was always left unlocked, so he slipped into the sanctuary and sat down in the second pew, laying his head down on his hands on the back of the pew in front of him.

He was ashamed that he had hurt Clare by his silence. She was such a dear friend, so genuine and good. And lovely. And funny. And generous. But, even if he loved her as a man should love a woman, he knew there was something about that idea that didn't fit. He didn't know what it was, but something was holding him back and he didn't know if it was a leading from the Holy Spirit, or something else entirely.

Next week he had an appointment with the Christian counselor Martin had recommended. According to his friend, the man had worked with numerous pastors and seemed to have a gift for helping them. While James had no doubt that God sometimes chose to use other believers to accomplish his work, he believed even more, with all of his being, that it would be God's work, and not man's, to flood him with the truth and the cleansing and the power to overcome this present difficulty.

And so, throughout the night, he prayed. Then, just before the dark began to give way to the faint glow of morning's light, he stretched out on the pew and slept.

Twenty-Five

Tuesday
August 25

On the Tuesday following Sophie's birthday party, Bo was waiting in the prison chapel when James arrived. It was obvious Bo wanted to hear all about the party and James was happy to oblige, sharing all the details about the afternoon, from beginning to end, including Sophie's delight over the Barbie dolls and accessories which were Bo's gift in absentia. Katrina had also sent with James several Polaroid instant pictures from the party to give to Bo.

While the younger man pored over the photos, James was remembering the trip downtown with Clare to pick out the gifts and her unexpected declaration. He still couldn't understand why he was unable to speak or move or respond to her in any way. He should have at least opened his mouth and expressed to her how grateful he was for her friendship, even if that was all he felt.

For no reason, the previous evening around the dinner table came into his mind. The new boarder, Mr. English, was most agreeable and, some would say, extremely handsome. There were two ladies boarding with Clare, one in her early twenties and the second a retired schoolteacher. Both they and Clare had seemed to smile an inordinate amount since Mr. English's arrival and the smiles were usually aimed in that gentleman's general direction. Well, James was happy those fine ladies were receiving the attention of such a refined fellow. Yes, that was all he was feeling about that. Happy for the ladies.

"Preacher James," Bo interrupted James' reverie.

"Hmm?" James pulled his thoughts back to the present.

"Have you heard anything about a company wanting to buy land around the mountain top?"

"Yes. In fact, the company rep is staying at Clare's. Seems a nice enough fellow."

"Oh. It just doesn't make sense to me. What do they want with that land?"

"I understand they want to build a resort."

"That land's no good for a resort." Bo's years of business experience took over and he lost the unassuming attitude he usually wore around James. "You need to be cautious, Preacher. Don't make any decisions without having some confirmation of the facts from a reliable outside source. Just don't sound right to me."

James took Bo's advice seriously. "Thanks, Bo. I'll do exactly that." After all, Bo had years of dealing in property and sales and profits. In that respect, Bo was the expert and James knew he was the novice, thanks to his years of incarceration. So when Bo spoke about those subjects, James listened.

Twenty-Six

"So you see, Miss Canfield, this is more than just an opportunity for you to enjoy the wealth that is yours but not currently accessible. It is a chance for you to do something wonderful for your community. The kind of project the Stockton Corporation is planning is beneficial in every conceivable way."

Thelma shifted in her seat, but remained attentive. Mr. English seemed to be a sincere man and she wanted to hear him out, but her knees were telling her in a most unpleasant way that rain was imminent.

He continued, "It's good for the local economy, good for local people, providing jobs and business opportunities, and from an environmental standpoint, there could be no safer way to preserve the natural resources and beauty of the area, than by creating a resort that makes so little impact on the environment while guaranteeing the preservation of, well, practically the whole mountain.

Tom paused to gauge her reaction. Thelma's expression had not changed, not since the small, tight smile of greeting upon his arrival. Perhaps he had overloaded this simple woman with too much information too fast.

"Is there anything you'd like to ask me?" he inquired politely.

Except for a few blinks, her face was motionless.

"Would you like me to go over the financial aspects of the offer again?"

This time her gaze broke away toward the stairs and stayed there for a moment.

"No, sir," she answered firmly. "You can leave all those papers. I'll have to do some serious thinking about all this."

"Absolutely, as well you should. Selling your home is a major decision. However, we would appreciate having your answer within two weeks. The company is also considering a second location for the resort. If we can't confirm positive responses of at least eighty percent from you and your neighbors, Heaven's Mountain could lose this opportunity."

When Mr. English had gone, Thelma hobbled to the suite of rooms that were formerly occupied by Miss Sadie, Billy's grandmother. Miss Sadie had been Thelma's employer, but more importantly, her dearest friend. Thelma had left the rooms as they had always been, filled with Miss Sadie's personal treasures.

From the bedside table, she took Miss Sadie's Bible, carefully marked throughout with notes and underlines. Taking her time she sat down in the cushioned rocker, holding the Bible in her lap. She had shut the door when she came in. She wasn't one to care what anyone thought, but still, she didn't want folks thinking she was batty, talking out loud to herself and God, and sometimes even to Miss Sadie. The talking helped her get her thinking straight.

Today there was a lot to think about. The offer for her property was fair. She was pretty sure about that. But she had always thought that this place would be her home, and Billy's home, too, as long as he wanted it to be. And then there was Katherine to think about.

"Oh, Lord, thou knowest my every thought, so you know what's on my mind. I love this place. Mostly because of Miss Sadie. Makes me feel close to her. But you heard Katherine last night, didn't you, Lord? She's such a smart girl, and good, too. She's thinking about law school and that's going to cost a pretty penny. I've had the money to help her with college. You know I'm the only one she's got that is able to help her. But I don't have enough for law school, and I'd hate for her not to

Mountain Girl

go just on account of the money. If I sold the house and land, I could help her."

Still as stone, she sat and thought. Then, "You want me to just wait a while, Lord?" The clock on the mantle clicked softly.

"Okay, Lord. That's what I'll do." Placing her work-worn hands on those arthritic knees, she pushed herself up. On the way out, she patted the door. "I miss you, Miss Sadie."

Twenty-Seven

"Give me the keys, Billy," Kate warned, reaching behind him as he toyed with her, knowing full well that he could aggravate her to the point of exasperation if he wanted to. "I'm driving this time."

"Nope," said he, switching hands and holding the keys out to the other side. "You're worse than Thelma, poking along like an old, worn-out plow horse. I'll drive."

"Come on, Billy. You've got your own car. You drive all the time," she whined.

Billy hesitated a second too long and she grabbed the keys.

"Get in, Buddy-ro," she said, with a smug look his way. She got in and slid the seat back a bit to accommodate her long legs. "You have the list, right?"

"Yeah, yeah, I've got the list. I don't know why I've got to come along at all. You and Thelma could have done this yourselves," he grumbled as he climbed in.

"Hush, Billy! You know Aunt Thelma's knees have been hurting all week. There's no way she can go walking around that grocery store for an hour."

"Yeah, I guess. But why do you need me?" It was Billy doing the whining now. "You could go by yourself. You are, after all, an intelligent college student, aren't you?"

"Yes, I am. A rising junior as a matter of fact. Unlike another, who shall remain nameless, who could also have his first two years behind him if he hadn't goofed off the whole first year." Her voice rose a little as she emphasized her displeasure over his irresponsibility.

"Hey, hey, now. Water over the bridge, right?" He flashed a charming smile her way.

"Doesn't work any more, Billy Boy. Hasn't worked in a long time. Not since you did that thing to my boyfriend a couple of years ago," she said, in her best "offended" voice.

"Aw, Katie-girl. Aren't you ever going to let that go? Besides, the guy wasn't hurt. He just got wet." Billy got back out of the car and slammed his door shut, muttering under his breath.

"What did you say?" demanded Kate.

"I said he was a jerk anyway. You deserve a lot better."

Somewhat mollified by the compliment, she agreed. "Well, yes, he was a jerk." Then she gave him a dirty look. "But so were you."

He looked through the car window and gave her a sugar sweet smile. "So, Kate, will you forgive me?"

She rolled her eyes. "Just get back in the car," she said and then, knowing how he hated it, "*William.*"

Twenty-Eight

"You don't mind fixing up this bedroom for Mom, do you, Ethan?"

"No, I don't mind a bit." He manhandled a filing cabinet into the far corner of the room then turned and surveyed his work. "I should have done this a couple of months ago. Your mother is going to want to spend those first weeks after the baby comes right here with you." He smiled without reservation at his pregnant wife, in spite of the fact that Grace's last minute change of heart about her mom's sleeping arrangements had required that he reschedule several appointments this morning. "There. Hand me those sheets and I'll make up the bed for you."

"Hey! I'm pregnant, not disabled, you know." She bustled over with the sheets. "Besides, you've done enough to help me today. You go on and visit Mr. Osborne – tell him I hope he's feeling better – and I'll have dinner ready by the time you get home." She snapped a sheet into the air above the bed. As it was floating down onto the bed, he came up behind her and nuzzled her neck. She turned within his embrace and placed her arms across his shoulders.

He studied the look on her face. Her whole mind and heart was in that look, and it told him everything he needed to know.

Twenty-Nine

Wednesday
August 26

*I*n the far corner of the small home-town restaurant sat a handsome older man dressed in what had to be a designer suit. From the description Clare had given her, Grace had no doubt this was the Stockton Corporation's man, Tom English. Even though Grace now had several years of experience under her belt, she couldn't help feeling some trepidation at interviewing such a worldly looking gentleman.

He saw her now, and held up his hand in a friendly gesture. As she approached the table, he rose and extended his hand to her. "Mrs. MacEwen?"

"Yes. How do you do," she said politely. "Thank you for agreeing to meet me today, Mr. English."

He motioned her towards her seat, sliding it in for her in gentlemanly fashion. How very nice, she thought.

"You have received high accolades from every one at Miss Morgan's establishment, Mrs. MacEwen."

Smart, she thought. He was beginning with a compliment in order to get her guard down. Well, it would not change her agenda for today. She had chosen the restaurant setting, hoping that the smell and taste of excellent cuisine would allow him to feel relaxed and expansive.

Hopefully his refined New York palate could also appreciate some down-home southern cooking.

An hour later she had come to the conclusion that he was either a superb actor or that he was a genuinely nice guy who truly believed that his company was going to do great and good things for Heaven's Mountain.

Thirty

"Good morning, Ethan. Fill 'er up?"

"Good morning, Wally. Yes, please. Fill up and check the oil, too, while you're at it."

"Yes, sir," the gas station attendant answered smartly. He hurried to start the gas, then checked the oil, pulling the dip stick to show to Ethan, who nodded that it was okay. Wally began washing the windshield. "So, how's Mrs. MacEwen? It's almost time for that baby to come, isn't it?"

"She's doing real well, Wally. Thanks for asking. We've got a little more than three weeks to go," said Ethan.

Wally laughed and moved over to the passenger side windshield. "You think you've got three weeks, but it could be anytime now, Ethan. It could even end up being two or three weeks past her due date. These babies, they just pop out when they're ready to pop out." He gave the windshield a final swipe, then came over to top off the gas.

"Let me give you some advice, Ethan."

Ethan thought, *Oh, great, just what I need, yet more advice.* Aloud he said, "Lay it on me, Wally."

"My advice," said Wally, "is to keep your tank full and your oil checked. You never know. That little bundle of joy might decide to come in the middle of the night, all the gas stations are closed, and you've got to drive your wife, who is in labor, to Gainesville." Wally held up his hands, palms up. "And there you are, almost on empty. You see what I mean?" He put his arms down.

"I see what you mean, Wally."

"I rest my case. See you around, Ethan. Remember…"

"Keep my tank full. Got it."

Thirty-One

Grace had been looking out the window every few minutes, trying to catch sight of her mother's car the minute it arrived. She had given herself the afternoon off, so as soon as her lunch appointment with Mr. English was ended, she hurried home. Interrupting her vigil long enough to make some sweet tea, she was rewarded by the sound of gravel crunching in the driveway.

Opening the back door, she saw her mother, as usual, attempting to unload every item from the car and get it in the house in one trip. Every finger had hold of a handle of some sort.

"Here, Mom, let me help you."

"I've got it. I think I've got it. Hey, sugar!" she said, leaning over to hug her daughter, boxes and bags bouncing off of both of them. "Don't pick up anything heavy! Oh, look at you! You look great! Are you feeling good?"

Grace nodded. Inexplicably, she was tearing up again, but it was for a pleasant emotion this time, so she didn't mind. "I'm great, Mom. I'm so glad you're here." She watched as Nan tried to manhandle another paper grocery sack out of the back seat. "Oh, just leave some of that stuff, Mom. Ethan will bring it in for you when he gets home."

Reluctantly, Nan capitulated on her "one trip" rule, letting several straps slide off her arms. She grinned comically at Grace. "Just a habit. I can't stand to make two trips!"

"Come on." Grace grabbed her arm, hooking it through her own. "Ethan's rearranged the new guest room, which used to be his office, for you to stay in, so let's put your bags in there." She led the way down the hall and into the room. "I know you were just being nice when you said you wanted to stay with Clare. Not that you would mind staying with Clare, of course. But this room is yours as long as you want to stay."

"Oh, that's sweet of you and Ethan. I'll try not to get in your way, or interfere with your household – or with you and Ethan!"

"And don't you dare work yourself to death here. Mom, I mean it. I want this to be your own little mini-vacation, at least a little bit. You go visit Clare and cut up and have fun with her all you want to while you're here, okay?"

"Sure, sweetheart. I do think I'll wait until tomorrow to go see Clare. That drive tuckered me."

They were back in the hall and Nan pointed to the old guest room and said, "Is this the nursery?" She put her hand on the doorknob to peek in.

"No!" shrieked Grace. Letting go of the doorknob, Nan jumped back from the door and stared in shock at her daughter.

Grace was embarrassed. "I'm so sorry I yelled! It's just that I've been keeping it hidden from Clare, too, and I thought I'd show it to both of you tomorrow."

"Whew! You had me wondering…"

Thirty-Two

Thursday
August 27

Several days after their first jaunt, as Clare was washing the breakfast dishes, Tom stuck his head around the door. Clare looked up and smiled. He grinned back at her. "Could we go today?" he asked.

"Yes, sir. We sure can. What time?"

"You choose. I'm free all afternoon."

"Two o'clock? I need to be back at least by four thirty."

"Two it is. I won't be here for lunch, but I'll be here at two to pick you up."

"Great! I'll pack a light snack for us."

When he was gone, she repeated the words in her head, "I'll pick you up". Wow. That almost sounded like a real date! Was it?

She finished the breakfast clean-up, and started in on all of the dinner preparation that could be done ahead of time. She would put the roast, potatoes, onions and carrots in the oven on low at one-thirty. The evening's bread would be sliced sourdough, toasted with butter and garlic salt. And dessert would be easy-peasy instant chocolate pudding, with whipped cream on top. She could easily manage all that between four thirty and six.

She was busy cutting up all the vegetables when Grace and her mother, Nan, burst through the back door. "Here she is!" shouted Grace. "I told you I'd bring her over first thing this morning, and here we are!"

Clare threw down her knife and a half-peeled potato and hurried to hug her dear friend. She and Nan had met a couple of years earlier, when Grace first came to Heaven's Mountain hoping to solve a decades old murder. They shared an instant rapport, and now stayed in touch, writing or calling every few weeks.

"Clare, I'm so glad to see you. How long has it been, hon?" Nan still hadn't let go of Clare's neck.

"Too long," Clare mumbled. "Christmas?" They let go the hug, but held onto each other's hands.

"Yes, Christmas. Grace has been to see us several times since then, but it's been hard for me to get away. You know, Granny Annie broke her hip, so I haven't wanted to leave her for long."

"How is she doing now?"

"Much better. She's up and around on her own. But I moved her into the Big House with Augusta, and there's a full-time caregiver that's taking care of both of them while I'm gone." Nan reached over to include Grace in the next group hug. "I couldn't miss my baby's big moment!" Nan kissed Grace's cheek. "And I plan to stay at least two or three weeks after the baby gets here, too!"

"That's fantastic," Clare gushed. "You and I will have plenty of time to catch up, too."

Grace changed the subject. "So, what are you cooking, Clare?"

"Oh!" Clare hesitated only a millisecond before spilling the beans. "You know my new boarder, Mr. English? Tom?"

"Oh, so it's 'Tom', huh?" queried Grace.

"Yes, Miss Nosy, we call each other by our first names. We're friends."

Grace and Nan exchanged knowing looks.

Grace continued with her questions. "So, what does Tom have to do with the potatoes you're peeling?"

Clare gave up, drooping her shoulders in total submission. "Tom and I are going to take in the view up on Heaven's Mountain. This afternoon. So, I'm getting my supper done ahead of time, so that I can be gone this afternoon."

"Unh-huh. I see." Grace was using her tough reporter's look, her eyes squinting out a steely gaze.

"Clare! Is this a date?" Nan's eyes were wide with wonder.

Clare scrunched up her face, then opened one eye to look at her girlfriends. "Mmm. I don't know. Maybe?"

"Omigosh!" Nan squealed like a schoolgirl. "Why haven't you told me?"

"Yeah, Clare." Grace spoke in more serious tone. "What gives? I thought that…"

"No, no," said Clare, giving Grace a warning stare. Then more emphatically, "No!"

Nan looked from one to the other. "I don't know what's going on here, but you know you're going to have to 'fess up eventually. Right, Clare?"

"Okay, okay," she nodded. "Not today, though."

"All right, well, I guess we'll leave it at that," Grace conceded. "But only because I want you both to see the nursery before I have to go to work!"

"Now?" Clare looked doubtful, sparing a sideways glance at all those potatoes.

"Come on," begged Grace. "I wouldn't even let Mom peek last night, so I could show it to both of you at the same time…"

Clare looked flattered but still undecided until Nan spoke up. "Come on, Clare, it'll be fun. And I'll get Grace to bring me back over here so I can help you peel this gigantic pile of potatoes."

"All rightee, then," she acquiesced, taking off her apron. "Let's go see Baby MacEwen's new room!"

Thirty-Three

"Oh, how precious!"

"It's adorable."

Grace beamed with pride as Nan and Clare admired her handiwork in decorating the nursery. She and Ethan had spent several days painting and hanging curtains and pictures to create a Pooh theme. The results were magazine-worthy, she thought, in no small measure because of the baby bed, chest, changing table and rocker built by Jed Liles.

"Oooh, almost forgot! Open this!" Nan thrust a large package into her daughter's hands. "It's from Augusta. She was so upset that it wasn't ready in time for the shower last month."

Grace sat down heavily in the upholstered rocker Ethan had given her. "Oh, she shouldn't have worried over that." She snatched off the last bit of wrapping paper and slid her fingers around the edge of the lid to pop the tape loose.

"You're going to love this, Grace," her mother warned.

Grace lifted the top, then opened the tissue paper to reveal the treasures within, for there were several. She unfolded the tissue from the topmost package. Inside was a white christening gown, with delicate smocking and little pearl buttons, with an exquisite matching cap and tiny booties. After sufficient oooh-ing and aahh-ing and passing things around, the next gift was opened.

It was an outfit for a toddler, a navy blue and white sailor suit for a little boy, beautifully tailored and finished. This was also handed around, with the workmanship greatly admired.

The clothing items were separated from the other contents of the box by thick layers of more tissue. Grace dug down and pulled out two vaguely familiar photos in lovely formal frames. One was an infant in a christening gown identical to the one in the box. The second was of a little boy wearing the same sailor suit.

"Are these…?"

"Yes," Nan answered. "Augusta had the two outfits made to exactly match the ones that your father was wearing in these two pictures. She tried to restore the original garments, but it couldn't be done, so she hired a professional seamstress to recreate them. And if it's a girl, she'll have a little dress made, nautical style to match the boy's sailor suit."

"This is so special," Grace said, her eyes beginning to water.

"She also said that she wants the baby's picture made in the outfits. She wants to pay for that, too, she said."

"Oh! Then we can hang them side by side! Oh, that will be perfect! Ladies, excuse me. I've got to call my grandmother."

Nan was leaning over the crib, rubbing her hand across the printed sheet. Clare came and stood beside her, placing an arm around her friend's shoulder.

"How do you think she's doing?" Clare asked.

"Grace? A little tired, maybe," Nan replied. "She's a very determined girl. She's made up her mind to work until her due date, and that's exactly what she'll do."

"Unless the baby comes early," remarked Clare.

"Unless the baby comes early," echoed Nan. "And I almost hope that precious stinker does come early," she admitted, "'cause I can hardly wait to get my hands on him!"

Thirty-Four

"Ready to go?" asked Tom

"Yes-sir-ree, bob!" answered Clare.

"I beg your pardon?"

"Oh. Never mind, just a childish expression." She felt a little embarrassed that she had used such a silly figure of speech. His use of the English language was so impeccable. "Here's the picnic basket," she said, handing it over to Tom, who placed it in the small trunk of the convertible. She had brought a scarf this time, to keep her hair in some semblance of order, as the wind whipped around with the convertible top down.

From the time the car left the driveway, they fell into an easy conversation. Though their backgrounds were very different, Clare truly enjoyed his company, and the feeling appeared to be mutual. Whether it would ever be anything more, she couldn't begin to guess, but she knew she had made a new friend.

"How is your work going, Tom?"

"Hmmm. How shall I say this? Not as smoothly as I had hoped."

"How so?"

Tom took a moment to answer. "I underestimated the emotional attachment these mountain property owners have for their land. Stockton is offering a generous price per acre."

Clare considered his comment. "It probably wouldn't matter how generous the offer is. Some of them have been on this mountain for generations. That means everything to them."

"I'm beginning to understand."

"Exactly what kind of development does the Corporation have in mind?"

"They plan to build a huge resort. Five star accommodations and dining. Spa facilities. Convention capabilities. Skiing. Equine boarding."

"Why here? I don't think a ski resort is possible, anyway. Our winter temperatures are not cold enough. The elevation is not high enough. Do they realize that?"

"You're not the first person to express that opinion to me. I have passed that information on to my employer, but so far, they haven't changed their plans." There was no lapse in the conversation as they headed up the mountain, passing the Lucas place, Heaven's Mountain Church, and the Canfield place. They were not far from the summit, when Clare sat up straighter.

"We're getting close now, so slow down," she instructed. "It's hard to see. Here. Turn here."

"Where?" Tom had stopped in the middle of the road.

Clare chuckled. "It's a good thing you brought me along. Right there, it's a dirt road. Go slow. There might be some potholes."

"Might be?" Tom shook his head, as he maneuvered slowly down the overgrown trail.

"If I remember right, it gets better after this first little bit. But, we can still back out. Want to wait until we can borrow a truck?"

"No, I'm an adventurer at heart. Let's keep going."

Another twenty yards and the way improved immensely. Still, they were hugging the side of the mountain with little room to spare as the other shoulder dropped steeply. Tom drove carefully and Clare kept a close watch on their position. Only a few minutes later, they came to

Mountain Girl

a large flat area, with boulders scattered along the edge, leaving an astounding view open for almost one hundred and eighty degrees. They were close to the top of the mountain and it was noticeably cooler than in town. They got out, turning round and round, trying to take it all in.

"This is magnificent," Tom admitted. "Reason enough to build a resort here."

"It tugs at your heart, doesn't it? God gave us a beautiful world."

"Yes, He did," agreed Tom. Catching her hand, he urged her forward, toward the biggest rock. "Let's sit down here for a while and enjoy this view."

For a long time Clare simply soaked up the warmth of the rock, the softness of the breeze and the feel of the sun on her face. With her eyes closed, leaning back on her elbows, she felt certain Tom was now watching her but she didn't really mind. It was actually pretty flattering. Finally her eyes opened and met his. Neither spoke for several seconds. Clare was thinking – again - about what a nice looking man he was. It then occurred to her that that wasn't a very deep or intimate or passionate thought to be having about a man who was about to kiss her. Still, the afternoon was so pleasant and Tom was such a nice fellow. And, most significant of all, there was no one else in her life right now to whom she owed any loyalty. So, when he leaned toward her, cautiously, gauging her response before advancing further, she moved ever so slightly and met his lips with her own.

Like the day and the man, the kiss was pleasant. Afterwards she smiled kindly at him, not wanting him to sense the lack of passion the moment inspired. By the time she retrieved the picnic basket from the car, things were back to normal between them. Just two friends, enjoying a lovely afternoon together.

By three-thirty, the winds had grown stronger and colder, so they packed up and started back, putting the top back up on the convertible because of the drop in temperature. Their talk was lively and teasing again. Having already shared with Tom details of her own childhood, Clare began a determined campaign to hear some of his childhood shenanigans. She didn't realize how distracted he had become, trying to respond to her silliness in kind, until they headed into the tightest curve on the mountain road at a dangerously high speed. Tom realized his mistake almost as soon as Clare did, and did his best to correct the situation, but it was too late. The car slid off the shoulder of the road and down the steep embankment, its progress soon halted by the thick hardwoods that covered the hillside.

Clare remembered Tom falling on top of her, despite the seatbelts they both wore, and an excruciating pain in her lower leg as the car bounced against a large oak. Then, nothing.

Thirty-Five

"You're not finished already, are you?" asked Thelma. Earlier, when she mentioned hiring someone to sweep the leaves and pine straw off the roof, Billy had volunteered for the job.

"Whew! Yeah, all done." He took off his t-shirt and wiped the perspiration from his face. "It's hot up on that roof."

Thelma got up from the table where she had been peeling apples, and took a pitcher of tea from the refrigerator. "Well, sit down a minute and cool off." She placed a tall glass of iced tea on the table. "How about a ham sandwich?"

"Ooh, yeah, with one of those good tomatoes on it." He took a long swig of tea. "Better make it two."

A few minutes later, a plate of ham sandwiches was deposited in front of him. As he chowed down, she resumed peeling apples.

After his immediate hunger was soothed, he slowed down a bit, enough to carry on a conversation.

"Hey, Thelma, have you heard about that guy who's going around trying to buy up the whole mountain?"

"I've not only heard about him. I've talked to him." She proceeded to tell him all about the visit from Mr. English, all the while watching closely to measure his reaction. She anticipated that he would be very territorial.

"You're not going to give it to them, are you?"

"I haven't decided anything at all. I'm just pondering it."

"Well." He jumped up and began pacing around the table. "You can't sell it. This is our home. Yours and mine. We're the only ones left."

She could have pointed out that he still had his father, albeit in prison, and his little sister, whom he adored, but she wisely did not argue the point with him. She just nodded. He was going to need a little more time to adjust to the possibility before she discussed the issue any further.

Changing the subject, she said, "Let's have some fried trout tomorrow night. I've been hankering for some lately. Why don't you and Katherine go fishing this evening?"

Before Billy could answer, the phone rang. He picked up the receiver and, stretching the cord across the kitchen, handed it to Thelma. While she talked, he went out on the screened porch and pushed back and forth in the porch swing.

A few minutes later, she followed him and eased into a rocking chair. "Did you know there was a wreck a little while ago, just a ways past the church? In that bad curve?"

He sat up and shook his head. "No, ma'am. Today?"

She nodded. "Mr. English and Miss Clare... But they're both going to be all right."

"That's good. I like Miss Clare."

"Go find Katherine and tell her to come here. We're going to go see if we can help with anything."

Thirty-Six

"Clare? Clare, can you hear me?" The familiar voice seeped through the black fog that covered Clare's consciousness. "Clare?"

There. She was out of the darkness now. She knew she was lying down and that she should open her eyes. She just didn't quite feel like it yet. She sank back down into the undemanding blankness.

When she heard her name called the next time, she was ready. She knew that voice. Her eyelids fluttered and then stayed open just enough to allow her to see the owner of the voice. "James," she whispered.

"I'm here. How do you feel?"

"I don't know. Sleepy." She tried to open her eyes wider. "Where am I?"

"You're in the hospital, but you're going to be fine," he assured her. "Your leg was broken and it required surgery to set the bone right." He grimaced a bit. "They had to put a couple of screws in, too."

"That sounds really gross." She attempted a laugh, but fell short. "Doesn't hurt right now." She closed her eyes again.

"You're still under the effects of the anesthesia…" The words faded away as she fell asleep again.

At the boarding house, the retired schoolteacher and a timid younger lady had determined that they, although admittedly not very experienced as cooks, were the best qualified of all the boarders to attempt putting a meal on the table that evening. They were trying to decide on a menu that would not be too demanding when Thelma and Kate arrived on the scene with Billy in tow, and everyone gathered together in the living area.

"How is she?" the boarders wanted to know. It was obvious their concern was real.

Thelma answered, "She's got a broke leg and it's going to take some time to get back on her feet, but she's going to be fine."

"I heard she was with Mr. English," another spoke. "Is he all right?"
"He seemed like a nice fellow," said someone else.

"He's going to be all right, too," Thelma assured them. "He has some broke ribs and a concussion. He just needs time to heal, too."

"Well, can we do anything to help?" asked the teacher.

An older gentleman chimed in, "Yes, we don't want Miss Clare worrying about us."

Thelma again took charge. "You all might need to do a little here and there, but my niece and I will be around every day to get the cleaning done, and Miss Nan – that's Miss Clare's good friend - will be doing most of the cooking. We'll help her out with that, too, whenever she needs us. Right now we're fixin' to start supper and it'll be on the table shortly."

Kate added, "Miss Nan said she would probably stay here for a few days. Right, Aunt Thelma?"

"That's right. But not tonight. Tonight, they're all gonna stay up there at the hospital, just to be close by."

The young lady commented, "I guess Preacher James is up there, too, to render what comfort he can to Miss Clare."

Thirty-Seven

Friday
August 28

Mmm, wasn't that a good night's sleep? Clare sighed contentedly and was going to roll onto her side, but her left leg was too heavy to move. She straightened back up on to her back and her eyes opened fully for the first time since the accident.

The first thing she saw was James, asleep in a chair by her bed, in what appeared to be an impossibly uncomfortable position. He must have heard her rustling the bed covers because he jumped and his eyes flew open.

"You're awake," said James.

Clare studied the room. "I'm in the hospital," she stated as James nodded in confirmation. "Why?"

"Your leg was broken." He waited for any indication that she remembered. "In the accident." Nothing yet. "On the mountain yesterday. You were in the car with Mr. English."

The memories surfaced, one piece at the time. "We went to see the view at the top of the mountain. It was beautiful. Then..." She was about to reveal the fact that Tom had kissed her, but that was private, she decided. "Then... coming back down the mountain, we took the curve too fast.... I remember the crash, but then I must have blacked out."

James took her hand and enclosed it with both of his. "I was just leaving my house when you drove by. A few seconds later I heard the crash. I came and found you."

She realized James had not mentioned Tom yet. She was afraid to hear what he might have to say but she had to know. "Tom...?"

"Broken ribs. Concussion. His wrist is broken, and there was some bleeding and bruising internally, but they think he's past the critical stage."

Relief shone on her face and she didn't notice the sadness that flitted across James' countenance because he managed to cover it up quickly. He let go of her hand and laid it gently back down on the bedcovers.

At that moment, the nurse entered to take vital signs, with Grace close on her heels with a big bouquet of black-eyed Susans.

"These are from Ethan and me and Mom," she said, placing them on the window sill next to several other arrangements. "Hi, James. How do you feel, Clare?"

"I think I'm okay. I haven't actually looked at my leg yet, though." The nurse placed a thermometer in her mouth, effectively ending her response for the moment.

"Clare, I'm going to go now. Grace, I'll see you and Ethan at dinner tonight." He hugged Grace and waved goodbye to Clare as he left the room.

"Now, let's see who these other flowers are from," said the ever-inquisitive Grace. "These pink carnations are from Tom. Very pretty." She turned to raise her eyebrows at Clare, as if to ask what was going on in that quarter. "I know they're from him because I placed the order for him last night. Since he has no family down here Ethan and I stayed with him until he went to sleep." She watched Clare for any reaction, but with the thermometer in her mouth, all she could do was nod. Grace continued to watch as she added, "We didn't need to stay with you because, except when you were in surgery, James didn't leave your side throughout the entire evening and last night." Clare's eyes opened wide in surprise. Satisfied, Grace went on. "And this potted plant is from Thelma, Billy and Kate. And by the way, don't worry about the boarding house. Mom is handling the kitchen, and Thelma and Kate are taking care of the housekeeping."

The thermometer was removed now. "Oh, bless their hearts! You know, I had not even spared a thought for my house; I'm still trying to take this all in, and remember how I got here."

"You don't remember the accident?"

"Vaguely. I'm pretty sure I passed out when the car hit a tree, but it seems like I should remember something after that. Something between then and now."

"Well, don't worry too much about it now. It probably doesn't matter anyway."

"While you're here, Grace, would you check on Tom for me? He must be okay if he's up to sending flowers, I guess." She waited for a nosy remark from Grace about her interest in Tom. None came.

"Sure, I'll do that right now." As she was leaving the room, friends from church were coming in, loaded down with more flowers, magazines, and food. Before long, the room seemed more like a lively hen-party venue than a hospital room for the sick or injured.

Thirty-Eight

James was in his room, working on his sermon for Sunday, though he was finding it hard to concentrate. For one thing, he had been up most of the night, staying at the hospital with Clare until just a few hours ago. For another, he was wrestling with the impact of Clare's words to him while they were at the accident scene waiting for the ambulance to arrive. Tom had been unconscious the entire time, but Clare had been in and out, and in her lucid moments she had talked to him.

With a feeling of urgency, James had been examining all the gamut of emotions he had experienced the day before, trying to make sense of them. They were strong emotions, unsettling, and he needed to understand.

It started when he saw Clare and Tom cruising by the old Lucas place in that sporty car of Tom's. James had been there most of the day, building new cabinets for the kitchen, but was leaving, sitting at the end of the drive waiting to pull out into the road. When they came past, even though the top was up on the Camaro, he could see enough to tell that they were laughing.

The sight of them made something well up in him. He just wasn't sure what it was. Was it sadness? Possibly. Disappointment? Maybe. Jealousy? Surely not.

He was still sitting in his truck at the end of the drive, wondering why he felt so rotten, when he heard the crash. He knew it had to be them. Slinging dirt and gravel out onto the road, he floored the gas, slowing only when necessary to navigate the curves. Only now, later, was he able to consider what he felt when he heard the crash. It was fear, most definitely fear. He was afraid of the worst, that Clare might have been killed in the accident. And that was perfectly normal, wasn't it? He and Clare had become good friends in the last two years. Close friends, in fact, able to talk about almost everything.

There was one more huge wave of emotion that day. When he got to the Camaro and could see that they were both alive but unconscious, he felt overwhelmed with… something else. Something that made him carefully take Clare's hand and bring it to his face and kiss it gently. That must have been relief on his part, relief to find them alive. Just relief, right?

He had waved down the next car, sending them to get help, then went back to sit by Clare. Tom was more or less in the driver's seat, moaning occasionally, but otherwise not responsive to James' questions about his injuries. James had opened Clare's door and was kneeling beside it, holding her hand, when she gasped and her eyes opened a narrow slit. "James," she breathed.

Without warning, his throat constricted, and he had to force out the words, "I'm here, Clare."

"I knew you'd come, James."

He didn't know what to say except to repeat, "I'm here."

"You know….." and her voice trailed off.

"What, Clare?" But she seemed to be out again, so when he heard the sirens he went back up to the road to help them navigate the way to the crash site. He didn't know that she roused once again to finish the thought, "You know….I love you, James…."

Thirty Nine

"Good morning, Miss Morgan. How do you feel today?"

"Good morning, Doctor Teal. I think my leg is feeling better today, but…"

"Chills and fever last night?" The doctor was examining the leg as he spoke.

"I think so. I feel very tired today."

"After surgery, this is not uncommon. I'm going to start you on an antibiotic and I'm afraid you're going to have to stay with us another day or two, just to be sure it's working as it should. Any questions?"

"No, I guess not." She was obviously disappointed. "I was hoping to go home today, but…"

"I know. This is not where you want to be," he sympathized, "But it should only be a couple more days and then you can go home."

"Billy, go clean that upstairs bathroom. Here's the Comet."

That young man turned around to stare incredulously at his cohort. "Have you lost your mind?"

"What?" Kate came back, reeking pure innocence. "We've all got to do our part."

"Uh, right. Cleaning bathrooms is not my part. My part is outside, raking and cutting grass."

Her eyes narrowed as she glared at him. "Laziness is a sin, William Lucas. Did you know that?"

"Oh, good golly Miss Molly! Kate, you are a hard woman." He glared back at her.

"How many times has Miss Clare done something nice for you, Billy?" she demanded. "Aunt Thelma told me how she catered your prom breakfast for you, and wouldn't take any money for it. And how she taught you those dance steps so you wouldn't make a fool of yourself at your first college dance. And how she...."

"Okay, okay," he said, snatching up the Comet as he passed by. "I'm going."

He really is a good guy, she thought, as she watched him climb the stairs.

Forty

"What a drag!" Clare said later to Nan. "I'm not used to just sitting around. By the way, thanks for bringing my crocheting. Maybe that will keep my mind occupied for a while."

"Glad to do it."

"Have you seen Tom today?"

"I did. I popped in to see him before I came here. He's doing very well. The doctor said he could go home – to the boarding house – not to New York. He's not supposed to travel for at least two weeks."

"Oh, Nan, that's going to be even more extra work for you, isn't it?"

"Oh, fiddle-faddle! Not enough to even mention. And Tom is so nice. Such a gentleman. I'm sure it will be no problem at all. Anyway, I told him he could ride back to the boarding house with me whenever he's ready."

"Well, I feel bad enough that you're having to spend all your time doing my work, instead of taking care of Grace. That's what you came here for, after all."

"How well do you know my daughter?" Nan raised one eyebrow. "I assure you, she does not need or want me to take care of her. I'm here for the birth of my first grandchild."

"Speaking of which, what did Grace's doctor say? Didn't she have an appointment yesterday?"

"Yep. Everything is good. No dilation yet, so I'm hoping the baby will come right around the due date, three weeks from now."

"Oooh, that's so exciting! Thank goodness, I'll be out of here and back to normal by then, and you won't have to worry about a single thing having to do with that boarding house."

Nan lowered her voice into that "serious girl-talk" tone and confided, "Do you know, I have really enjoyed being just the cook for a change? I've always cooked for Augusta, of course, but she wants the same thing every week. So boring! But this? This has actually been fun!"

"You're kidding."

"No, I'm not. Clare, I will fill in for you anytime you want to take some time off. You just let me know."

"Am I interrupting, ladies?" Tom's elegant voice broke in.

"Not at all, Mr. English," said Nan. "In fact, I'm going to leave you two alone while I bring the car around. I'll just wait for you in the patient dismissal area, Mr. English." She told Clare goodbye then slipped out of the room as a nurse pushed Tom's wheelchair over to the bed.

"I'm so glad to see you're all right, Tom," said Clare.

"I'm happy to see you looking so well, too. I couldn't leave this place without stopping by to see you first."

"I'll be back in a few minutes, Mr. English," said the nurse, closing the door quietly behind her.

"I'm so - " he began.

"Tom, I - " she said.

Clare giggled. "You first."

"All right," he spoke seriously. "Clare, I am so sorry this happened. It was my fault for driving too fast and carelessly, and now you're suffering because of my error."

"Oh, now, Tom. Don't you go trying to take all the blame on yourself. I should have been paying attention too, instead of running my mouth, distracting you." Clare held out her hand and he took it. "Now, I don't want to hear another word about it. You hear me, Tom?"

"You are a very gracious woman, Clare Morgan," he said quietly. He kissed her hand, then leaned over and kissed her on the forehead.

From where he stood, with the door cracked open, James had a clear view of the kiss on the hand, but with Tom's back blocking his line of sight, he assumed that the second kiss was a true romantic kiss on the lips. Another jolt of heady emotion smacked him in the gut. He let the door slide shut and walked away.

Forty-One

"Wait, Mr. English. Don't try to get out on your own. I'll come around and keep you steady." Nan was on chauffeur duty, having offered to drive the visitor home from the hospital. His beautiful Camaro had not survived the wreck, and was now parked in the tow company's lot, awaiting transport to the scrap yard, its final resting place.

Grimacing as he twisted around in the front seat of the car, he placed his feet on the ground and apologized, "I'm sorry to be so much trouble to you, Mrs. Turner."

"It's no trouble at all, Mr. English." She took his arm as he stood. "And it's 'Miss', not 'Mrs.'," she corrected him. Now why had she even said that, she wondered. How silly of her! Just because the gentleman in question looked a lot like Cary Grant was no reason to go all flibbertigibbet, for heaven's sake. Besides, she would never, ever consider being involved with a fellow who was dating one of her dear friends and Clare did seem to genuinely care about him.

"Take your time now," she said, as he put a foot on the front steps. "Hold onto the rail."

He stopped on the second step and grabbed his side, which was bandaged tightly. "Woo! One little wrong move and it feels like a knife is sticking into me." He tried to smile but only succeeded in presenting a wan, hopeless look.

Holding his other arm firmly, in a kind voice she reassured him, "We've got all the time in the world. We'll wait right here until it passes, all right?"

"Yes," he whispered, his breaths short and shallow.

In an effort to fill the time and distract him from his discomfort, she commented, "Clare keeps such lovely flowers here on the porch. Whatever the season, I've never been here that she didn't have something blooming. It's so cheerful, don't you think?"

His only answer was to nod in agreement.

"Especially the impatiens. The colors she chose really complement the white siding on the house." She looked back at Mr. English to see how he was faring.

His smile was only a little strained. "Yes, they do." He breathed in, then out, carefully. "I think I can manage the rest of the steps now." He explained his strategy. "I'll attempt to keep my torso as still as possible and just move my legs."

Demonstrating, he slowly lifted his left leg to the next step, then raised his body rigidly up, with Nan providing balance. "That worked!" Now the brilliance of his full-on smile washed over Nan.

Unable to stop herself, she smiled widely in return. "Well, let's do this then." Together they maneuvered the remaining steps without incident.

Nan held the front door open wide as he made his way gingerly across the wooden porch.

He stood just inside the door as she came inside and let the screen door swing shut. "I need to call my office before I go up those stairs. Once I ascend, I may not be able to descend," he joked.

Nan hesitated. "Well… We kind of thought of that already. We moved your things down into the back bedroom on this floor." She hastened to explain. "It's not as big or well furnished as your room upstairs, but…"

He interrupted, "Say no more." His expression was one of pure gratitude. "I thank you. So very thoughtful of you – or Clare – or whoever it was!"

"Clare's idea, my execution," she laughed. "Why don't you rest in here," she indicated the communal living area, "make your phone call, and I'll come back in about fifteen minutes to help you to your room. You should rest some before lunch."

"Again, thank you. You are most gracious." He lowered himself with care into a large stuffed armchair, took a moment to gather his thoughts, then picked up the phone to place the call to the New York office. They were not going to be happy.

Mr. English was right. They were not happy and they were sending a replacement. Temporary, so they said, as long as he returned to his duties within one week. Otherwise, the replacement would be permanent.

While the conversation progressed, he maintained his usual cool composure, but when he placed the receiver back in its cradle, he had to admit he felt a slight irritation. He wasn't worried about losing the position. His finances were in good order, and in fact, he only worked when he so chose.

He certainly didn't require to be fussed over, but a modicum of at least feigned concern for his health and well-being would have been in order. Strange folks, those Stockton chaps. Not for the first time since his employment began, he found himself questioning their development scheme, as well as their methods of land acquisition. Strange folks, he thought, as he drifted off into a welcome sleep.

Forty-Two

Sunday
August 30

*A*utumn is just around the corner, thought James, standing on the stoop of the church's front door. In keeping with a long-standing tradition, the Heaven's Mountain Church was now on its summer schedule, with Sunday services starting an hour earlier. He had to agree, it made for a more pleasant worship experience, for even here near the top of the mountain, the midday heat could be sweltering.

He enjoyed the quiet of Sunday morning in the house of the Lord, before anyone else arrived. Ever since his younger days, before prison, it had always been one of his favorite times to talk with his Father. This morning he had spent an hour at the altar asking that his spirit find peace and a resolution to the continuing disturbing dreams about Betty, the latest being just last night. Now, he was sure he felt a new calmness about that issue.

Clare's recovery had been on his mind ever since the wreck. He took time to lift her up for continued improvement. He missed his good friend and he prayed that she would find happiness with her new-found love.

He had also asked the Father for healing for the attacks of panic, where he seemed to lose all control over his ability to respond normally.

He wasn't sure about the answer to that prayer. Though he might wish for a different answer, right now it seemed that the answer was "wait".

From his stance on the porch, James saw the first members of the small congregation coming around the curve in their old Ford sedan. Diggy parked in the shade then went around the car to open the door for his wife. Right behind them came Miss Sally. Within the next ten minutes, the rest of the Sunday worshippers came through the door. All told, this Sunday's attendance came to twenty-seven souls, mostly older folks, with a few younger family members mixed in for good measure.

The church no longer boasted a piano, so James' strong baritone led the way through several hymns. Many in the congregation knew how to sing shaped notes, so the harmony was rich and full-bodied, enthusiastic if not always perfectly pitched. His foot tapping time, James finished off the last chorus with gusto, then motioned for everyone to sit.

"The sermon this morning is about trusting God." He paused for a moment to let the rustling die down, as people got themselves situated to sit still for a while. "What does that mean? What does it mean to you, to trust God?

"Are there people in your life that you trust? Do you trust your relatives?" He chuckled, "Hopefully you can trust some or all of them. Do you trust your friends? If you don't, are they really your friends?

"Would you trust them to take care of you if you couldn't take care of yourself? Would you trust them to be on your side when you needed them? Would you trust them to take over all your possessions and do the right thing with them?"

"Let's turn in our Bibles to the story of Joseph first, then a little later we're going to talk about that most complex story, the story of Job."

James read from the book of Genesis then began to expound on the scriptures. "So everything was taken away from Joseph. First of all, his family. He no longer got to be with his father and his mother and his brothers. Next, his possessions. Everything was gone, all the luxuries he was used to. Even that rich, fancy coat of many colors of which he was probably so proud. When he was taken away by that caravan, there was no one on Joseph's side. He had no one and no things.

"But for someone so young, Joseph was brilliant with wisdom. How? In what way, you ask?" James stopped to look around the room before making his point. "He was brilliant…..because……he trusted God.

"Joseph was sold into slavery. He could have been bitter about that twist of circumstances in his life. But he wasn't. He could have turned away from righteousness, given up on the precepts learned at his father's knee. But he didn't. He could have felt so betrayed by all the people and all the rules that he had trusted all his life that he could have decided to never trust anyone or anything again, not even God. But he chose not to go down that road, dear friends.

"Joseph didn't give up on God. In spite of everything that happened to that young fellow, he put his life in God's hands and he trusted that God had an overriding purpose for whatever circumstance he found himself in. He believed that God would see him through whatever the world threw his way, and he just kept on doing what was right.

"He was treated unjustly. But he forgave his brothers who had betrayed him." Unbidden, James' thoughts went to his own wrongful conviction. He pushed the thought from his mind and continued. "He didn't get to live the life he probably thought he was going to live, with his family close by and with wealth and power at his disposal." Again, the similarity with his own sorrow and disappointment at being ripped from the life he should have had bore down on him. He felt the panic take hold, and rushed to finish before he lost the ability to speak at all. "But Joseph still chose to trust God and do what was right." He made a final effort and gasped out, "Diggy, would you lead us in the benediction?"

Though the old deputy was obviously surprised by the preacher's request, he complied. As the first words of the benediction were spoken, James hurried out the side door by the pulpit, leaving the complexities of Job for another Sunday.

Forty-Three

"It's just chicken and dumplings," Nan reiterated.

"Well, it's wonderful," Mr. English insisted. "Somehow I actually feel comforted by this dish," he said as he dug into his second helping. The other boarders had already excused themselves and only Mr. English and Nan remained at the dining room table.

"It's my mother's recipe," said Nan, obviously pleased by the compliment. "She began teaching me to cook when I was quite young."

"You learned well," he said. He wiped his mouth with the napkin and stretched back in his chair. "Miss Turner, would you mind calling me by my given name? This seems very formal, as pleasant as our relationship has become."

"With pleasure, Tom, if you will call me 'Nan'."

"Of course. Nan. So, how old were you when you began cooking?"

"Hmmm. I think I made my first biscuits when I was five."

"Astounding."

"Of course, I'm not sure anyone *ate* them," she laughed, "but I did pat them out myself."

"And did your daughter inherit your culinary gift?"

"Grace." Nan nodded. "When she wants to, Grace can outcook me any day of the week, but her interest lies elsewhere. Her passion is writing."

"I've heard from several sources that she's quite good."

"She is," confirmed her mother. "And, I've been told, a skilled 'investigative reporter' – I believe that's the proper job title."

"It wouldn't seem that there would be much need for investigative reporting in such a lovely small town as this," he remarked. He prepared to rise, placing his hand over his ribs. "I suppose I must spend some time catching up on my paperwork, since I have been out of commission for several days. I hate to end our conversation, though. It's been a pleasure, Nan."

"For me also, Tom."

He bowed his head slightly and walked stiffly, slowly from the dining room. Thoughtfully, she watched him go.

Forty-Four

Monday
August 31

Unlike the previous Monday, Grace was happy to hear from Joe today. "Hey, Boss. How's the weather in Myrtle Beach?"

"It's fantastic. This week has been so great, I wish we could stay two more weeks instead of just one. If Jack didn't have to start back to school the day after Labor Day, I'd seriously consider it."

"Oh, Joe, don't even think that!" she replied. Grace didn't want to be whiny or weak, and she certainly didn't want to manipulate her boss with guilt over leaving an eight month pregnant woman to manage everything (after all, he did try to get her to call Ed), but she absolutely couldn't handle an additional week. Trying to keep it light, she said jokingly, "I can see it now – top story next week – Interim Newspaper Editor Delivers Baby in the Stacks and Goes Right Back to Work - Full Story on page 3."

"Oh, don't worry," he assured her. "I'll be back - right on schedule. Seriously, Grace, how are you holding up? You sound a little stressed. We can still call Ed, you know."

"I'm all right, Joe, just tired," she admitted. "I'll be fine." She gave him a quick update on what was making news in town, in particular the accident involving Clare and Mr. English. "Which brings me to the Stockton Corporation. I checked for any new permits at the courthouse.

Came up empty. Also, I'll be talking to Mr. English again tomorrow, although I don't really expect to get anything new out of him. He's home from the hospital, but he's pretty much out of commission for a while."

"Well, hold on to your seat, 'cause I've got some good stuff for you concerning Stockton. You know my buddy from school?"

"Yeah, did he find something?"

"He says Stockton is currently under investigation by the SEC for insider trading, plus there are lawsuits pending against the company which allege that they violated federal and state statutes by making false statements for the purpose of obtaining permits for strip mining. He says it's likely they'll be filing for bankruptcy within the next few months unless they get a major cash infusion and quickly."

"Oh, wow! Joe, that's unreal. So, how much of that is verifiable and good to print?" They discussed which parts could be confirmed by second sources and who Grace could contact for more details. It was going to mean a lot of overtime over the next few days. "Joe, there's one thing that we still don't know, and that is, are they really planning a resort, or is that a front for something else? If it is a ruse, what are they really up to and why do they want all these options?"

"My gut tells me there is no resort, but beyond that, I have no idea. Hey, what was your impression of their company rep?"

"He's a very likeable, old-world charm kind of guy. He didn't strike me as the deceitful type. Should I tell him what you just told me and see what his reaction is?"

"I don't see how it could hurt anything. It might stir up the waters a little, and we can just see what floats to the surface."

"Will do, Boss. Anything else you want me to do?"

"Just be sure you don't overdo it, Grace. Call Ed if you need some help. You promise me you will?"

"Yes. I promise I'll call him if it gets to be too much."

Two days after Tom's dismissal from the hospital, at 3:00 p.m., Mr. Reithoffer arrived at the boarding house to meet with him. The replacement agent had decided that the mountain town of Fairmount could not possibly provide for his extensive personal needs, so he had opted to maintain a room in the largest hotel in Gainesville, still woefully inadequate compared to New York's amenities.

In anticipation of his arrival, Nan had prepared the sunroom for their use, since it could be closed off for privacy and provided a table and chairs at which they could spread out their materials.

The meeting lasted over an hour. Nan noticed that when the two emerged, Reithoffer's steely expression appeared unchanged, while Tom looked disturbed and slightly flustered. She kept her observations to herself and did not ask any questions.

Forty-Five

The waiting room was empty. As he took a seat in a straight chair, James was relieved that he would not need to smile or talk with anyone. He was uncomfortable enough about this appointment with a counselor. In fact, he had started several times to cancel the appointment, but something always held him back.

He wasn't sure that he should be here at all. Shouldn't a pastor have enough faith and a close enough relationship with God to handle anything? And his problems were so very small compared to all the blessings in his life, he felt ashamed to be asking for more.

"Mr. MacEwen?" The soft voice of the secretary at the door interrupted his troubled thoughts. "You want to come on back?"

He managed a nod and a small smile for the young woman. She led him down a short hall to the last door on the left, then stepped back to let him enter. A tall, gangly man was rounding the corner of the desk, his arm stretched out to grasp James' hand.

"Come in, James. May I call you 'James'?"

"Please do."

"My name is Mitch Brown. Let's sit over here." He motioned to two low armchairs covered in flowered fabric. "Would you like a cup of coffee?"

"Umm. Yes, thank you." James felt himself relaxing a little at the normalcy of the visit so far.

In fact the next twenty minutes were so normal that James almost forgot the purpose of the meeting. Mitch was so genuinely kind and interested that James knew that whatever else was happening, he was getting to know a new friend.

"So what's going on with you that made you come to see me?"

There it was. The Question. James felt a flash of anxiety. Could he reveal the moments of fear and panic, the sensation of numbness and the inability to respond. Could this man help him? Within his thoughts, James prayed. And then he talked.

I should go by and see Clare, thought James. I haven't seen her since Saturday. He was feeling a little washed out after his first counseling session, and would have preferred to simply go home and to bed. However, he had to admit his reluctance was also due to the turmoil he experienced when he witnessed the parting kiss between Clare and Mr. English on Saturday. Still, a friend did not neglect a friend in need simply to maintain his own comfort level. Therefore he would do his duty and visit Clare in the hospital.

She was sleeping when he got to her room. Not wanting to disturb her, he sat down in a chair, picked up a newspaper and began reading.

"James?" The sweet voice floated into his mind, piercing his consciousness and ending his afternoon nap. He rubbed his eyes, then peered over at Clare, who had on her usual merry face. How ever does she do that, he wondered.

"You're looking very well," he said.

"I'm feeling much better," she affirmed. "In fact, I'm way past ready to go home!"

James laughed. "I bet you are. All of the boarders send you their best."

Clare motioned toward the counter at the window. "They sent me that huge pot of bronze mums. Aren't they lovely?"

"Well, they all miss you. Nan is doing a wonderful job on the cooking, by the way. Actually, she seems to be having a ball," he chuckled. "I've only been around my fellow "in-law" a few times, but I've never seen her so happy and talkative. Cooking must agree with her."

"Are Thelma and Kate still coming every day?"

"Except for yesterday, Sunday, yes. Everything's spic and span."

"I'm so blessed to have good friends," said Clare. "Like you, James."

"No more blessed than I am to have your friendship, Clare." *Let it rest at that, Clare*, he thought. But she didn't.

"James, I…. Things have been a little awkward between us lately. Well, ever since I…"

"I know," he interrupted. He wanted to apologize, or say something that would make things go back to the way they were. He missed the easy camaraderie he'd had with Clare. But that could be no more, now that she had Tom. "Have you spoken to Tom today? He's doing better, getting up and around a little more."

Clare seemed confused by the abrupt change of subject. "Yes, he called this morning."

"Well, I really should go. Bye, Clare."

Forty-Six

Clare watched him practically run out of the room, her heart breaking to see him so distraught. He didn't even say a prayer with her, for her quick recovery, a standard ritual for a pastor visiting the sick. No matter, she would pray for him instead this time. He seemed to be in need.

"Father, I lift James, your beloved servant, up to you. I don't know why he's hurting, but my prayer is that he will feel Your presence, and that whatever is troubling him, he will trust you and turn it over to you. Please give him discernment so that he can deal with whatever it is. And place in his path those who can give him aid and edify him. Thank you for all the blessings you bestow on us, Lord, but especially for the blessing of good friends. I thank you for all my friends who are carrying me right now and I pray that you will bless them beyond measure. I love you, Father. In Jesus name I pray, Amen."

At eight o'clock that evening, back in the shadows of the hardwoods at the City Park, a man hid just inside the tree line, waiting. Fifteen minutes passed and since there was no moon, dusk passed into full dark.

Then headlights appeared, swishing back and forth down the curvy entrance road, coming to a halt by the gazebo.

Treading lightly across the expanse of grass, the man who had been waiting approached the parked car. For several minutes the figure inside the car spoke, while the one who stood nodded every now and then. A fat envelope was passed from within the car and grabbed by the other man, who stuffed it quickly into his pocket. After nodding once or twice more, he slunk away, back into the shadows, and the headlights flashed against the trees as the car left the park.

Forty Seven

Tuesday
September 1

The drive to the prison Tuesday morning found James turning over in his mind the previous day's conversation with Dr. Brown. He had surprised himself with the things he had said. It was as if a dam had burst and his words and thoughts could not be held back, but came rushing unchecked out of his mouth. Deep, hidden feelings that had to be dredged up as from a muddy bottom were strangely imbued with wings and were flying loose all through the atmosphere. Nothing was solved or fixed, but he noticed that his mood somehow felt lighter today.

As he passed the prison gate, he expected the usual fleeting drop of his stomach, but it never came. First time ever, he thought. That was encouraging.

Perhaps the clarity in his thoughts and the calmness in his spirit had an effect on everyone around him for the chapel service was especially Spirit-filled this morning, with testimonies gushing out through cracks in otherwise hardened shells.

After the meeting was over, James and Bo were stacking up hymnals and Bibles when a young man's voice called out from the back of the room, "Whoa, Preacher James, you're in the groove today!"

"God is always in the groove," was James' comeback. "Have we met?" James cocked his head in thought and gave the boy the once over.

"No, sir, but… uh…," the young fellow in prison stripes seemed ashamed and ducked his head. "I…uh… think you've heard of me. I'm Darrell."

"Ah, yes," said James, "I believe I've met your father."

"Yes, sir. I'm sorry if he was out of the way with you."

"Think nothing of it, Darrell," James assured him. "Trust me, I've heard much worse than that."

"Yeah, I guess so. You were in here almost thirty years, so I heard."

"That's right."

"And you still believe God is good?" Darrell appeared doubtful.

"Absolutely. He was with me every minute I was in here. With me every minute now that I'm out."

The guard in the back of the room cleared his throat. "Guess I got to go," said Darrell. "Nice talkin' to you, Preacher."

"Good to meet you, Darrell."

Bo had been advanced to trustee status, so he stayed behind after Darrell left. "Not meaning to pry, Preacher, but has ole' Gus been giving you any trouble?"

James shrugged. "Not really. Nothing to speak of. He approached me in the park a week or so ago. Tried to scare me off from talking to Darrell. Actually, I didn't know who Darrell was until today."

"That Gus is a sorry thing. Mean as the devil. It's sort of amazing Darrell hasn't completely taken after him. At least it doesn't seem that way."

"The boy does seem to have some potential. I'm glad he's coming to services. God would make a world of difference in his life."

"I'm proof of that, yes, sir." Bo raised his brows and gave James a stern look. "Now, I know I don't need to tell you that his daddy is a crazy old coot, and apt to do anything when he's boozed up or angry, do I?"

"No, Bo, but I appreciate your concern just the same."

Bo picked up his own Bible and walked to the door. "You watch yourself around him, James. Don't be alone with him. Safer around other people, 'cause he's really a coward at heart."

"Bo, I'll keep that in mind. God bless you, son."

Forty-Eight

Mr. Reithoffer knocked on the door as if he already had possession of the small white frame house. A neatly dressed older man with a cane answered the door. "Can I he'p you?" he asked politely.

"Yes, sir, you can. May I come in?" Mr. Reithoffer went immediately into his pushy salesman mode. "I've brought some papers for you to sign. Simply a formality, really. All the landowners in this area are signing options offered by my company. We believe that you and your family deserve the services and amenities that are available in a less isolated setting. I'm referring to fire protection, emergency medical services, animal control, and of course access to libraries, shopping and governmental offices, all within a reasonable distance of your home."

The man motioned for Mr. Reithoffer to take a seat on the plastic-covered sofa. As the plastic crinkled and crackled, Mr. Reithoffer continued, "Now, what we are offering is a generous option figure, yours to keep if my company decides not to exercise it, and in the event that the option is exercised, you will receive a payment that far exceeds the current fair market value of your property."

Satisfied that he had made a definite impression on the backwoods mountain fellow, Mr. Reithoffer held out the clipboarded form and a pen and said, "Now, if I can just get you to sign on this line, right here…."

Jacalyn Wilson

The backwoods mountain fellow looked at the papers and the pen and then up at Mr. Reithoffer. "What the heck are you talkin' about? I'm not signin' anything unless my lawyer reads it first."

And so the day went for the Stockton Corporation's new man, house after house, pretty much the same response. One could almost feel sorry for the man. Almost.

Forty-Nine

When Grace parked in front of the boarding house, Mr. English was waiting for her. He was sitting in one of the large white wicker chairs, with pillows stuffed all around him. She doubted that he could move, and wondered who had helped him get situated in that fashion.

"You look like you're feeling better," Grace greeted him as she sat down in the porch swing.

"Thank you. I do feel better. As long as I'm careful and don't make any sudden movements, I'm actually feeling very well."

"I'm glad. Clare is coming home today, isn't she?"

"Yes, she is. Probably a little later this afternoon."

Time to get down to business now, thought Grace. "Thank you for agreeing to meet with me again in an 'official' capacity. Not quite the same as visiting you in the hospital, is it?"

"I don't mind a bit, Mrs. MacEwen."

"Okay, then. Mr. English, some things have been brought to light about the company for whom you're working, the Stockton Corporation, from what we believe is a very reliable source. I'd like to tell you what we've discovered, and if you have any comments, we'd be very interested to hear them. Is that all right with you?"

Mr. English nodded. "Proceed."

"We have confirmed that the Stockton Corporation is currently under investigation by the Securities and Exchange Commission for insider trading, and distributing misleading prospectus statements." Grace paused.

"I was not aware of that," Mr. English commented.

She went on to the next item. "It is our understanding that the company has pending lawsuits relating to fraudulent statements made on permit applications for strip mining." She paused again.

"I was not aware of that, either," he said.

"Mr. English, have you seen any detailed architectural renderings of the proposed resort?"

"No, just the basic layout included in the presentation folder. I think you have seen those."

"Yes, I did see them. Did you actually see the feasibility study report that was supposed to have been prepared by the outside firm, Randall and Ripshaw?"

"No, I never saw the report. The study was simply mentioned in the presentation."

"In your opinion, do you think the Stockton Corporation is actually planning to build a resort on Heaven's Mountain?"

Mr. English hesitated, then answered cautiously, "I did believe it. Now, quite frankly, I am not so sure."

Fifty

"Dinner was.." James kissed his fingertips then threw his hand wide in an expressive flourish, "perfecto!" He rose from the table and went around to pull out Grace's chair. "Now. No arguments, young lady. Your husband and I are going to clean up the kitchen, while you put your feet up and rest." Grace looked from one to the other. "Go." With more relief than resignation, she kissed them both soundly on the cheek and waddled away.

While James took up a position at the sink, Ethan cleared things away. "How's the house coming, Dad?"

"Oh, slow right now."

"How come?"

James shrugged. He wasn't yet ready to confide in anyone, not even his son, concerning the counseling sessions with Dr. Brown. Besides, Ethan had enough to deal with right now, with an emotional pregnant wife and a job offer on the table. "Several church members sick over the last couple of weeks. And…I just haven't been in the mood lately."

Ethan began drying the dishes in the drainer. "Everything okay, Dad?"

"Sure. Everything's fine. Why?"

"You've just seemed a little preoccupied lately."

"Nothing to worry about." He handed a dripping platter to Ethan. "What about Harry Carroll's offer? Have you made a decision yet?"

Ethan sighed, "No, I haven't. I have one month to decide, or rather, I *had* one month. Just a little over two weeks left now." He took the frying pan James was holding out to him. "I haven't felt a definite leading either way. Grace is usually the ideal sounding board, but I've had…, we've had difficulty communicating lately about several things – this being one of them."

"Hmm. Big changes are coming into your lives soon. You could both be a little apprehensive and not even know it. Plus, Grace has all these physical challenges to contend with, not the least of which is the imminent delivery of a baby."

"Is all this as danger-ridden as folks are telling me?"

"What ever do you mean?"

"Well, I have people telling me every day – all kinds of things! Swollen feet, premature delivery, post-partum depression, no sleep, diseases the baby could have that we have to watch for." Ethan fell into a chair and slumped forward. "And what if we don't make it to the hospital in time? I don't know how to deliver a baby!"

"Ethan, Ethan, son…" His own worries faded away as James put his arms around his son and settled into just being a father.

Fifty-One

Wednesday
September 2

"Are you sure you want to do this?" asked Nan.

"Please, yes! I can't stand it another day," begged Clare.

"It doesn't look as bad as you think," Nan assured her friend.

Clare shivered in disgust. "Maybe not, but it feels nasty."

Clare was balancing on her crutches in front of the kitchen sink, her head bent far over, as Nan used the sprayer to soak her hair.

"Are you okay on those crutches? I'm going to do this as fast as I can so we can get you off that leg." Quickly, she lathered and rinsed, lathered and rinsed, with Clare moaning the whole time, "Oh, that feels so good. Oh, yeah, that feels great."

Putting the sprayer back into its socket, Nan ordered, "All done, but be still. Let me put this towel around your hair." With that mission accomplished, Clare adjusted the crutches and led the way to her sitting room just off the kitchen.

Holding on to her friend, Nan kept her steady as Clare got settled on the couch. Nan placed a pillow under the leg which was in a cast. "How's that?"

"That's better than wonderful." Clare sighed contentedly. The day before, all the rigmarole required to get out of the hospital and get home had exhausted her, so today was the first day she could actually enjoy being at home.

"You want me to roll your hair or just dry it?" asked Nan.

"I think I can roll it myself, if you'll just get my rollers from under the bathroom sink."

Nan went obediently to get the rollers. From the back, she yelled, "Picks or bobbie pins?"

"Picks."

After Nan got all the paraphernalia arranged just right within the reach of Clare's arms, she settled herself in a comfy arm chair facing Clare. "So. Clare. It's time to 'fess up, girlfriend. I want all the scoop on you and Tom."

Clare was thankful she had a mouthful of picks just then because it gave her a moment to think. Should she share everything with Nan or keep it to herself? Or maybe share only a part of it? Several times before in her life she'd been badly burned from trusting someone with confidential matters that she didn't want repeated.

For all her merry ways and outgoing personality Clare was actually very cautious about revealing too much of her innermost feelings and thoughts. But this was Nan. And she knew this friend well enough to know that she would never betray her.

She took the last pin from her mouth and stuck it through a roller. Choosing the next size smaller roller, she separated another strand of hair and began winding. "Well-l-l-l," with her hands still up above her head Clare gave Nan an impish look and bit her lower lip.

"Oh, boy, this is gonna be good!" Nan rubbed her hands together. "Wait! For something this momentous we're gonna need some coffee and some of that chocolate cake I baked this morning. You roll fast and I'll get the goodies. Then we're going to sit down and have a serious "revelation conversation".

Clare just rolled her eyes and said, "Go get the cake. You're gonna need that chocolate."

"Ooooh, better and better," Nan teased as she danced her way across the room and into the kitchen.

Mountain Girl

Five minutes later the hair was rolled, the cake served and the coffee poured. Nan tucked her legs beneath her in the big armchair and took a sip of her coffee. "Okay, spill it." And then before Clare could answer, Nan blurted, "It's Tom, isn't it? I just knew it. Clare, he is absolutely gorgeous! And such a gentleman. And a man of the world, too."

Clare finally interrupted, "He is all that, and that's the truth. And we did enjoy a nice afternoon together…"

Nan was clearly bewildered by Clare's tone of voice. "And…?"

"And there was one, very little, kiss in there somewhere." Nan was still silent, waiting for the rest. Clare finished, "And that was all. We're just friends."

"But it can develop into more than friendship…" she urged.

"Mmmmm. No, it can't," Clare said decisively. "There's not going to be more."

"Aw, Clare, I'm sorry. He's such a nice guy."

"Yes, he is a catch," Clare agreed. "But….gosh, I don't know if I should even be talking about this, but if I don't talk to somebody I think I'll just bust, and you are my dear friend…" Clare's voice broke.

"Oh, honey, what is it?" Nan put down her coffee and came over to put an arm around her.

Clare cleared her throat to stop the wayward tears that were threatening to trickle out. Where to begin? "For quite a while now, I've had feelings for someone else, but…he doesn't feel that way about me, evidently." Clare laughed a self-deprecating chuckle. "Among other things, it's quite a blow to my ego."

"Well!" huffed Nan, "He must not have good sense, Clare! What did he say?"

"He didn't say anything. Literally! I, uh, got real courageous, or else real foolish, one night and told him how I felt, and he said nothing." She turned a sad face to Nan. "I've never been so embarassed in my life."

Nan said seriously, "You've prayed about it, haven't you?" Clare nodded. "Is the Spirit leading you toward this man, or are you sensing a check in your spirit?"

"I'm not feeling that God wants me to give up or to move in a different direction."

"Sounds like it may be a matter of waiting – for his feelings to catch up with yours?"

"Right now, that's the way it seems to me," agreed Clare.

"I'm assuming, for whatever reason and because you have not mentioned his name, you would rather I not know the identity of this man?"

Clare shrugged. "I don't want you to act any differently around him. And you might not be able to help it, if I tell you."

Nan turned a knowing smile on her. "Do you really think I can't figure it out? I know you pretty well, Clare, and I've seen the way you look at James – like you think he's the most wonderful thing since sliced bread, and like you could just eat him up."

Clare's shoulders slumped in surrender and she shook her head. "A girl just cannot have a secret around here, can she?"

Fifty-Two

While Nan and Clare were having a pleasant tete-a-tete, Mr. Reithoffer and Mr. English were in the sunroom conducting a meeting of a different sort.

It had been almost a week since the accident and, while he was by no means pain-free, Tom was feeling more like his old self. The purpose of today's meeting was to share information and compare actual results to the company's goals and projections, but Tom had his own personal agenda planned.

He suspected that Mr. Reithoffer's knowledge of the Stockton Corporation's true plans far exceeded his own, and he believed it was time for him to become privy to some of that knowledge. Grace Turner, the reporter for the local newspaper had asked him some thought-provoking questions yesterday, questions to which he had no answers, and he did not like being in that position.

In deference to his tender ribs, Mr. English had arrived early so that he could get himself settled comfortably with a pillow braced against his side. It probably was not the powerful image he would have preferred to project, but it would have to do. Anyway, he had confidence in his own ability to control a meeting. Besides that, he knew Mr. Reithoffer's kind.

He was basically a hired thug, one who, if pressed in the right way, could be compelled to reveal the coward he really was.

"Good. You're here," was Reithoffer's greeting as he bustled in with his briefcase in tow. He slammed it on the table, popped it open and drew out several folders. "I don't know what you've told these people, but apparently it was not conducive to finalizing our business here."

"I've given them the information that was given to me by the corporate office. Wasn't that what I was hired to do?"

"You don't have to tell them anything, English. Just get them to sign, that's all."

"Well, maybe if I had known a little more about this project I could have served the Stockton Corporation's interests a little better. Are we not promoting the development of a five star mountain retreat?"

"Sure." Mr. Reithoffer sounded almost sarcastic. "But right now we just want the options on the land. That's all."

"It seems to me that if Stockton is going to undertake a project that will require many years to bring to fruition, it would be in the company's best interest to foster a spirit of cooperation and goodwill with the local people. You cannot bully these people around and engender their goodwill."

Mr. Reithoffer looked exasperated. He huffed, "We don't care about their goodwill." Then, seeming to think better of it, he added, "Not at this time, anyway. We'll worry about that later. Right now, we just want these options signed, as many as we can get.." Thumbing through the papers in his briefcase, he located a large map and spread it out on the table. "Now, show me again which properties you've already covered."

Mr. English took a pencil and circled the areas he had visited the previous week. Quite nonchalantly he inquired, "What's our deadline for getting the options signed?"

"Four days from now. Sunday night."

Satisfied, Tom smiled a little to himself. That should be enough to narrow the field substantially.

Fifty-Three

When Mr. Reithoffer was gone, Tom went to find Nan, who was in the kitchen making biscuits. She was humming a lively old four part gospel hymn, and she was swapping back and forth, humming first one part and then another. Tom had never heard anything like it before, so he held back at the door and watched her, humming and patting biscuits, a thoroughly lovely sight even with the smudge of flour on her chin.

She finished filling the second cookie sheet with biscuits, popped them in the oven and turned around to see what needed to be done next. When she spotted Tom at the door, she was startled but recovered quickly. "Well, hello there. What are you up to, Tom?"

"I admit I was watching you form the biscuits. I've never seen that done. I guess I thought they were all shaped or cut out by a machine."

"Maybe in New York, but not in Fairmount. In fact, I've got a little dough left over. Would you like to try it?"

He was reluctant, but intrigued. Curiosity won out. "All right. I'll do it!" He stepped up to the counter.

"Unh, unh!" Nan pointed to the sink. "First you wash your hands."

"Of course. Clean hands." He hastened to comply.

Holding up his now clean hands like a surgeon preparing to operate, Tom came to stand by Nan in front of the dough bowl. "What now?" he said.

"See the pile of flour here? Scoop up a large pinch and dust your fingers and palms. Be generous. Then cup your fingers around a golf-ball sized glob of dough."

"This much?"

"A little more. Yes, that's fine. Now, watch me and do as I do." Nan dusted her hands and got some dough. "Use your fingers and palms to pass the dough back and forth, rounding it as you go."

She watched as the dough clung to his fingers and wouldn't come loose. "Wait, you need some more flour." Using her free hand, she dumped a pile of flour on top of the dough in his hands. "Now, slowly, - don't let the flour spill out - let the flour be the shield between your hands and the dough. Watch me."

Nan expertly flipped her own biscuit back and forth, from one hand to the other, until it was a nice round pattie, then with her still floured hands, she eased it onto a small greased cast iron skillet and pressed her fingers gently on top, making finger shaped ridges.

Once again, Tom attempted to imitate her movements. He did get the gooey dough into one ball, but the shaping did not go well.

"Okay, just shape it into a round ball," said Nan, taking another tack.

She spread some flour on the counter. "Now, lay it on here." He did as instructed and she sprinkled flour on top of the dough. Nan took an empty jelly jar, that was now used as a small drinking glass, from the cabinet. She rubbed flour on the outside of it, then told him, "Roll this across your dough to flatten it." When he was done, she said, "Now, flip your glass, and use the edge to cut out your biscuit. Like a cookie cutter," she smiled.

"Kind of like play-do," he smiled back.

"Put it in the skillet beside mine and flatten it gently with the back side of your fingers." Easing his creation into the pan, he looked at Nan for encouragement. "That's fine. Now press down." His biscuit now had ridges, too. "Way to go, Tom! We'll just pop these into the oven and they'll be ready in no time. Nothing like eating a biscuit that you've made yourself."

"You mean I have to eat it?"

Nan laughed. "We'll see how it turns out first!"

At the sink, he rinsed and dried his hands. "Actually, Nan, I did have another reason for visiting the kitchen, other than receiving a free biscuit-making lesson," he nodded appreciatively at her. "Do you have a phone number where I could reach your daughter? We talked yesterday and now some other things have come to my mind in which she might be interested."

"Sure thing. She's probably at home by now." Nan got a pad and wrote down the number. "If you don't want to use the house phone in the hall, go in the sunroom and shut the door. There's an extension in there."

Fifty-Four

"Law', come on in, Preacher James," said Miss Sally in a high-pitched querulous voice. She was holding on to the top of her housecoat, keeping it closed tightly. "I woulda been dressed a little nicer if I'da known you'uns was comin'." Miss Sally pushed the screen door open and stood aside so the preacher could enter.

"Why, you look lovely to me, ma'am," said James and was glad to see the twinkle in her eyes that said she still enjoyed a compliment even at her age. "I know I'm coming unannounced, so feel free to say so, if this is not a good time for me to visit."

"It's always a good time for you to visit, Preacher." Though not as refined and cultured as her late younger sister Sadie, Sally nevertheless shared the family virtue of hospitality. "Come on in now and set down. Here, take the chair by the stove, why don't you."

James could feel the heat and didn't know if he could stand it right by the stove. Like many an octogenarian, Miss Sally had a hard time keeping warm. Even this morning with the temperatures passing eighty and moving on toward ninety, she had her coal burning stove going. He decided it wouldn't hurt to ask.

"Miss Sally, it's such a beautiful day. Do you think we could sit outside on the porch?" He could tell she wasn't thrilled with that idea, but her gracious nature pushed her to agree.

"I reckon we could. It's still kinda chilly out there. I could put on my sweater." In her house shoes, she was shuffling toward her bedroom in the very back of the shotgun house when James had a twinge, no, more like a stab, of conscience, as a trickle of sweat ran down his back.

"Wait, Miss Sally. You know, I think we'll be fine in here. I'll just sit over here by the door in this rocking chair and you take the chair by the stove. That's your chair anyway, isn't it?"

"Yes, sir, it is. Kind of you to remember that that's my usual place." She settled herself in the straightback chair, just a foot away from the stove.

Even next to the door, with an occasional light breeze gliding past, James could now feel the perspiration dripping down both sides of his face and off his forehead, to lodge precariously in his eyebrows. *Best to make quick work of this visit*, he thought. Then, *for shame, James. You'll stay here as long as the Lord needs you to stay.* Yes, he would.

"I was worried that you might be sick, Miss Sally, when you weren't at church Sunday."

"I 'preciate you coming to check on me, but I wasn't sick, thank the Lord. My great-grandson was visiting my daughter, his grandmother, from Colorado. He made a special trip from Atlanta on Sunday, just to come and see me."

"How wonderful! How old is your great-grandson?"

"He is twenty-two years old and he is going to be a doctor! How about that? We've never had a doctor in our family, and he's going to be the first. Of course, the military is going to pay for him to go to school, so he'll have to serve for a number of years after, but that's all right. Only fair, I say."

The entire back of his shirt was soaked now. It has to be ninety degrees in here, he thought. "Ethan said you called the other day, and wanted to talk to me about the land development company."

"Yes, I did. What do you think about all this, Preacher?"

Mountain Girl

"I know it's a major decision for all of us, not to be made lightly or without an ample amount of consideration. Personally, I'm not planning on selling my property, but we all have to decide for ourselves."

"You like it up here, huh, Preacher?" she asked.

"Yes, I surely do. Very much. After all the work I've put into my place, I wouldn't want to lose it before I even get to enjoy it."

"How much longer before you move up here?"

"Not much longer. A week. Maybe two. The house is pretty much finished."

"I always loved that view from the Lucas place," Sally reminisced. "Best view on the whole mountaintop. 'Cept maybe the one at the lookout point, just a little above your place."

"I've extended the back porch. It's almost like another room."

"Lawsy-mercy, I'd love to see it."

"See it you shall, then. Once I get settled, I'll come and get you one day and we'll sit on my back porch and look at the view. How's that sound?"

The old woman clapped her hands together in pure joy. "Marvelous! You won't forget me now, will you?"

James stood, having to pull his damp pants legs loose from the slats of the chair. "No, ma'am. I promise I will not forget you."

When he walked back outside, it felt nice and cool, even though it was a hot August day. He had no other commitments, pastoral or otherwise, for the rest of the day, so he decided to spend it finishing up some minor jobs at his house.

A few hours later, James looked with satisfaction at his handiwork. The railing, the last unfinished part of the back porch, was now complete. A good day's work.

He had purchased a couple of old wooden rockers at a junk store and put them on his porch. He pulled one up close to the new rail and sat down and put his feet up. Life of Riley, for sure.

The silence was soon broken by the sharp crack of a shotgun, followed by three more shots in rapid succession. Not too far away, thought James. He stood up and walked over to the end of the porch, toward the direction from which the shots had come. From his vantage point, he could see Thelma's house and yard, the yard of the Wagners, her next door neighbors, and parts of several roads running along the mountainside and in the valley below. Probably somebody killing a snake, maybe a rattler.

He was about to return to his rocker when he caught a movement out of the corner of his eye. Zeroing in, he saw a flash of color. A man, walking fast, then running, across one of the county maintained roads. As James watched, the man ducked behind the cover of some trees, only to emerge a few seconds later in an old beat-up truck. Gus Woody! Now, what was that fellow up to? No good, no doubt.

Fifty-Five

Thursday
September 3

Dr. Brown had recommended that James come for another appointment the same week as his initial visit. James was more than willing, because even though nothing had actually changed – yet – he realized that he harbored a great many feelings that he had never shared with anyone and some that he had never examined himself, so it seemed a good thing to open up his emotions and allow an expert to assist him in dealing with them.

Mitch began, "Tell me about Betty. What was she like?"

"She was lovely," James answered, "in so many ways. She had an inner beauty, a calmness and sweetness about her. Even through all the disappointment and rough times, she was a peaceful, safe place for Ethan, and for me."

"Did she come to see you often?"

"Once a week. Never long enough for either of us. I think it was actually easier for me than for her, because she had to deal with providing for the family and she wasn't really equipped to do that. She was brought up to be a good wife and mother, and she was. But she did the best she could and never complained. All I had to deal with was losing my freedom."

"What about when she had cancer?"

"What do you mean?"

"How did you feel about her dying - without you there to care for her?"

"I felt awful. She had Ethan, of course, and she had many good friends, but it should have been my responsibility to take care of her."

"Would you say you feel guilty about that?"

"Yes. Yes, I would," James answered strongly.

"Let's dissect that for a minute," said Mitch. "If you were counseling someone as their pastor and they were suffering false guilt, what would you say to them?"

"Well, first we would talk about the situation that created that guilt feeling. And I would ask them two questions."

"The two questions would be…?"

"Did you do anything to cause or precipitate the situation? And is there anything you could have done to change things or to make things easier for the other person?"

"How would you answer those questions about Betty's illness and death?"

James took a minute to think. "I didn't cause it, and there was nothing I could have done from in prison that I wasn't already doing. So, why do I still feel regret?"

"You know with your intellect that you have nothing to feel guilty about, and yet you still find yourself feeling guilty. What would you tell someone else?"

"Depending on the situation, I might suggest the possibility that Satan is loading them up with false guilt, in which case, every time they have that feeling, they should reject it from their mind, bind his activity, and pray to know and feel only the truth which comes from God."

"So that's what I'm telling you. You have no blame in Betty's death. No blame whatsoever."

"So I need to take my own advice," countered James.

"Exactly! That's your homework for next time, to cast out that feeling and not let it back in."

James replied, "I can work on that."

"Good." Mitch continued, "Let's talk about that dream you keep having. What does it signify to you?"

"I don't know. That I want Betty and I can't find her? That she's gone?"

"Maybe. But there's probably a little more to it than that. Did you grieve when Betty died?"

"Yes, of course, I did."

"Was there some anger mixed in, maybe some bitterness that because of that rotten Beamon Lucas, you couldn't be there for your wife?"

James crossed and uncrossed his legs, agitated and moving restlessly. "It wasn't fair," he said, blinking rapidly. "It wasn't fair for Betty or for Ethan or for me. We didn't do anything wrong."

"No, you didn't," Mitch agreed. "Because of Beamon, your life, the life you deserved, was effectively stolen from you, wasn't it?"

James had placed a hand across his eyes, rubbing them. "Yes," he whispered.

"James, I want you to consider this possibility. Could it be that in your dream, you are wanting your old life back? Not just Betty, but your whole life? You're looking for it, trying to get it back, but you can't seem to hold on to it?"

"Mitch, I know that that life is over. I'm grateful, I really am, for the freedom and blessings I have now: I've been cleared of murder, I have my son, a daughter-in-law and a grandbaby on the way. I am a blessed man and I know it."

"Sometimes what we know and what we feel are not in sync. Sometimes we have to deal with our feelings before we can move forward and live in the truth."

"I don't know...."

"Think about it over the weekend. Allow yourself to experience whatever feelings are there. You can't deal with it until you do."

"More homework, huh?" James managed a weak smile.

Fifty-Six

"Come on, Katherine. Come with me," cajoled Billy.

"No!" she answered, clearly irritated. "I'm busy."

"You're just reading," he argued.

"It's required summer reading for the literature class I'm taking this fall. Leave me alone now." She went back to her book, burying her face in it.

"Seriously, Kate, you need to get a life. Anyway, the Wagners' dogs have been missing since yesterday. I told them we'd search our property down to where it ends at the power line."

Kate lowered the book. "The two golden retrievers, Sam and Senda?"

"Yeah." Here it comes, he thought. She's such an easy touch when it comes to animals.

"Well, why didn't you say so to start with?" She jumped up and slipped her shoes on. "Do you think we should take some bandages, maybe some mercurochrome? How about a wheelbarrow – or a wagon – in case they're hurt and can't walk?"

"No, let's just find them first. If we need anything, I'll run back up here and get it," he promised.

She was already out the door. "Let's go. What are you waiting for?"

They had about ten acres to cover, all hilly terrain and wooded. Two hours later, when they had canvassed about three-fourths of the area, they found the dogs. There were tied together with a rope which was knotted around a tree. At first, their golden color blended in so well with the leaves that Billy and Kate didn't see them. They were only about thirty feet away when the outlines became clear. Both of them knew right away that the gentle, fun-loving pets were beyond any help. They had both been shot.

Kate got down on the ground between them and rubbed her fingers through their fur, crying silently. Billy couldn't stand to see her so sad. In an uncharacteristically thoughtful way, he knelt down behind her and put his arm all the way around her neck, holding on to her shoulder. He began rocking her back and forth, murmuring, "I know, Katie-girl, I know. Shhh. Shhh."

A little later they were standing side by side looking down at Sam and Senda. Kate pulled up the tail of her shirt to wipe her eyes. "Why would anybody do this, Billy? Why? Who could have hated them so much?"

"Don't know," he mumbled. He turned his head away from her for a moment so she wouldn't see him swipe across his own eyes.

He took her hand and for once she didn't pull back or make a smart-aleck comment. "Come on, Kate. We've got to go tell the Wagners."

Numbly, no longer energetic and carefree, they began hiking across the hill toward the Wagners' place.

Fifty-Seven

In the cooling air of dusk, the front porch was quiet. James was in the swing, occasionally pushing off with one foot, making it glide gently back and forth. He was doing his homework.

Was it true? Was he punishing himself with guilt that was undeserved? Did he do anything of which he was ashamed? He could honestly say no. Though he would have given anything to have been there for Betty and Ethan, he was innocent of wrongdoing. Did he actually feel guilty though? He did feel a great sorrow and continuing burden for what they had to go through. But was that guilt?

He had counseled a number of people, both in and out of prison, who felt this same heavy sadness as part of their grieving, and it occurred to him that what he felt was grief. Grief over the loss of his wife, but more than that. Grief over the loss of those years of his life, grief over missing the birthdays and holidays and ballgames and times of intimacy with his family. He thought he had already passed through the grieving time for his wife, but maybe he had not yet accepted the loss of those years of his life.

He realized that he didn't want these feelings to color the rest of his life. And he was certain that his Father didn't want that either.

Mitch had also suggested that he might be harboring resentment over missing that normal life. Having come this far in seeking the truth, James went a little further. He admitted that it was true. He did feel some bitterness, usually well hidden, but there nevertheless, about the unfair circumstances that sent him away for years. He wanted resolution of these feelings. He wanted to be healed.

In the same way that he took his next breath, he began to pray, murmuring softly into the falling dark, his words rising and floating high as the fireflies glowing in the yard. *Gracious Lord, I've prayed every day about removing the effects of my prison years. I've wanted to be "normal" and to have had all the "normal" life experiences, such as other men my age have had. Thank you for showing me the resentment that has been coloring my life in the wrong way. Father, I loved Betty and she loved me, but I cannot serve you with my whole heart while my spirit continues to grieve. I hand these feelings over to you, and I'm going to take that wonderful love from my marriage and I'm going to set it in a special place of honor, but it's going to be a past blessing, to remember with joy, not a present grief or source of guilt. Thank you for taking this burden from me, Father.*

He stopped and listened for anything his Father might want to say to him. His mind wandered to his sermon preparation. He planned to finish the discussion from the previous Sunday, when he preached on Joseph. Now, there was a man who trusted God to use him for good. As he told his brothers when they came to seek his help, "You meant it for evil, but God meant it for good."

Why didn't he catch that before? Joseph didn't dwell on the past. He lived in the present and allowed God to use him. In fact, his past actually put him in the position to do the work God had for him to do. If he had lived his normal life, he would have missed the opportunity to do that work.

Oh, wow! Ever since his release, he had been looking at his life from the wrong perspective. Here he was, a pastor, and he had been blind to God's overriding purpose in his life. *Thank you, Father. Thank you for taking what was meant for evil in my life and using it for good. I'm having trouble letting go of that yearning for "normal" so help me grab hold of your overriding purpose for me and embrace it. I'm willing to work on this with you. Just show me how. Help me to live in the present, now, as you've revealed it to me.*

A long-absent peace was growing inside him. With joy, James felt its warmth. He sat still and quiet, enjoying the moment.

The screen door opened and Clare, still on crutches but somehow managing to hold onto a watering can, came out on the porch. On one foot, she leaned carefully over and poured water in each of the two big pots filled with impatiens. With a satisfied smile and an approving nod, she adjusted the crutches and slipped back inside, never knowing that James was there.

As full as James' heart was with his new-found peace with the past, he knew the emotion gripping him now was something else entirely. It was love for this wonderful woman.

Until this very moment, he had not realized what it was, and now he had let it slip right through his hands.

Fifty-Eight

At eight-thirty on Thursday evening, Ethan found himself at the Seven-Eleven praying that that establishment would be in possession of some butter pecan ice cream for his dear, sweet, finicky, just slightly demanding, pregnant wife. Compared to the cravings demonstrated by the expectant mothers on television, such as Lucy Ricardo and Laura Petrie, he was getting off easy, so he really wanted to deliver the goods on the few occasions when she did seem to desire a particular food or some other special attentions, like a foot rub or some rose scented bath oil beads. Tonight's fairly reasonable request just happened to be butter pecan ice cream.

There were few places in Fairmount that sold ice cream, and the A & P grocery had closed at eight, so this was Ethan's last chance to procure milady's pleasure. When he walked into the convenience store, several teenagers from the youth group were there, full of excitement about a trip to Lake Lanier the next morning. He talked to them a few minutes then moved off to the ice cream freezer in the back.

"Thank you, Lord," he murmured as he picked up the last round carton of butter pecan ice cream. He was getting his change from the clerk when he saw Diggy coming through the door. Ethan loved the old fellow, even though he could be a little aggravating sometimes, especially since Diggy thought Grace was the greatest thing since color tv, but tonight Ethan was in a hurry to get home to his wife, and he was not in the mood to listen to more of Diggy's well-meaning cautionary tales about pregnancy.

To that end, he said a brief hello and thought he was home free until Diggy turned right around and followed him back out the door of the Seven-Eleven.

Ethan just kept walking toward the car, in spite of Diggy's upraised finger and his raspy voice calling out, "Brother Ethan, I need to talk to you…"

"Some other time, Diggy. I'm in kind of a hurry tonight." Not waiting for a reply, Ethan slammed the car door and proceeded to pull away toward home and his adored wife, who had just five minutes ago crawled into bed and fallen fast asleep.

Fifty-Nine

Friday
September 4

"Katherine, this visit just wasn't long enough to suit me," Thelma said.

"Not long enough for me, either, Aunt Thelma. Would you hand me that stack of books?" Thelma handed them across the bed.

"Did you get that laundry that was in the dryer?" asked Thelma.

"Yes, ma'am." Katherine teased, "You already asked me that twice!"

"I'm sorry. Chalk it up to old age, child," said Thelma, only half-kidding. "Katherine, stop and listen to me a minute."

The young girl immediately stopped her packing and sat down on the side of the bed. "What is it?"

"I don't want you worrying about the money when you get ready to go to law school."

"Aunt Thelma, you've already helped me enough," Katherine protested.

"Well, I want to do it. You're my only living relative that's got a lick of sense and I'm glad to do it for you. Now I know law school is very expensive, a lot more than college. So, I've decided that, when the time comes, I'll just sell this big old place, and get me something more manageable."

"No, Aunt Thelma. No. I wouldn't let you do that, even if I did need it. I wish I'd known you were worrying about my law school money. The thing is, I think I may be in a good position to get a scholarship. The law school has a scholarship fund. Every year they give a scholarship to the offspring of a World War II Purple Heart recipient. And, though you may not remember, I am the offspring of a World War II Purple Heart recipient."

"But how…?"

"Dad! Can you believe it? Yeah, he did do one thing right in his life." She put her hand over her mouth. "I'm sorry. I shouldn't have said that. It was ugly of me."

Thelma agreed, "Yes, it was, but you're forgiven. Well, I'll be a monkey's uncle!"

"Aunt Thelma!" laughed Katherine.

"Well, it's just amazing sometimes how God provides, in ways we never expect! I guess I'll just stay right here then. That'll sure make Billy happy."

"Is this the famous world-renowned journalist, Ed the Magnificent?"

"And can this be that ace reporter, Grace MacEwen?"

"It is indeed. How are you, Ed?"

"I'm still pirouetting around my office whenever the notion strikes. The bigger question is, how are you? Aren't you due most any day now?"

"Almost. My due date is a little over two weeks away."

"Your mom is there already, right?"

"She's been here a week. We're all awaiting the arrival of Baby MacEwen. And thank you again for the Baby Journal you sent. I promise to make good use of it."

"I know you will, Ace. I've never seen anyone loves to tell a tale as much as you do, except maybe myself!"

"That's why I'm calling today, Ed. I'm trying to put together a story and I need some help."

"Whatever you need, Acie Gracie."

Mountain Girl

"Oh, you know I love it when you call me that! Anyway, here's what's happening...."

"Are you sure you've got everything?" asked Thelma.

"For the sixth time, Aunt Thelma, I'm positively, absolutely, emphatically sure!" Kate repeated.

"All right then. Billy, you've got your bag in the car?" demanded Thelma.

Billy held up the bag to show her.

"Well, I guess we're ready. Billy, I said you can drive, but the first time you sling me against the car door, going around a curve too fast, your license with me is suspended and Katherine will drive the rest of the way."

"Gotcha," answered Billy, already in the driver's seat.

Thelma instructed, "Katherine, you sit in the front with Billy. You know the way and besides, I don't think my heart can take it, watching him drive. Oh, mercy! We should have just made this a day trip, to take you back to college, Kate! What was I thinking?"

Katherine giggled and got in the front. When Thelma was settled in the back seat, Billy started the car. He had driven down the driveway and was about to pull out onto the paved road when Thelma stopped him.

"What did I do?" he said, turning around to look at her.

"Go back to the house," ordered Thelma.

"What for?"

"Just go back to the house," she insisted.

Billy maneuvered the car back up the narrow driveway and stopped. Thelma got out and went inside. A minute later she came back out, carrying her overnight bag.

Billy and Kate watched her get back in the car.

"Don't say a word. Just drive," she commanded, like a regal queen.

They managed to hold it in until they got on the road, then Billy and Kate burst out laughing, only to hear Thelma joining in from the back seat with a hearty guffaw of her own.

Sixty

The soft creaking of the porch swing was drowned out every few seconds by the laughter of the women floating through the kitchen window. Clare, Grace and Nan were handling the supper clean-up, though Nan had insisted on doing all of the strenuous labor. With her ankle in a cast, Clare had been instructed to stay off of it and keep it elevated, so she was sitting at the kitchen table drying dishes, while Grace was washing at the sink, perched sideways on a high kitchen stool so that her eight month pregnant belly could be accommodated.

Out on the porch, the menfolk were feeling contented and full. "I couldn't eat at Clare's table every day," said Ethan, leaning back in the swing and patting his stomach. "Grace is a wonderful cook, and my church ladies can put on a fine spread any day, but that chocolate pecan pie Clare made tonight was pure genius. If not for the fact that there were just enough pieces to go around, I believe I would have committed the sin of gluttony this evening."

James chuckled, as his son continued, "Seriously, Dad, how have you avoided putting on weight after living here for more than a year?"

"I suppose I can thank all those years of prison fare – never more than one helping of anything." James put his arm up along the back of the swing and got comfortable. "Now, if you want to, tell me how things are going with you and Grace."

Ethan rolled his eyes. "I don't know. One minute things seem fine. The next minute we're in the middle of another heated disagreement. Not exactly an argument, but a difference of opinion where neither of us seems capable of seeing the other's point of view. Any suggestions?"

"Well, I know you, and Grace, too, well enough to know that you've prayed about it." He looked inquiringly at Ethan.

"Yes, sir."

"Well, then. What exactly are you disagreeing about?"

"The job offer, for one thing. I'd really like to discuss it with Grace, but every time I bring it up, she says she is against me taking it, and she finds some excuse to leave the room or end the conversation."

"Hmm. That's just not like her, is it?"

"No. It's not. Do you…Do you think you could talk to her about it?"

James took his time answering. "I don't think that's a good idea. She hasn't approached me for my help. I would be intruding into her business."

"Yeah, you're right, I guess."

"Any other issues between you?"

"Well, there's the fact that she plans to go right back to work after the baby's born."

"Really? I thought she was going to take three or four months off."

"Well, right. Three or four months. But I don't want her to go back to work at all. It's not necessary. I can support us."

"I'm sure you could. What does Grace say?"

"She's afraid her skills will go stale if she doesn't work for the next fifteen or twenty years, until the children are about grown. But I told her, she could write on her own, when she has time. She could send her work to magazines, or write a book. I would have no objection to that."

"I see."

Ethan gave his father a puzzled look. "Mom never worked, so she was always there for me. That's what I want for my children."

"What makes you think your mother never worked?"

Mountain Girl

"Mom never had a job, Dad."

Eyebrows raised, James replied, "Oh, yes, she did. She was usually home by the time you got home from school, but she worked at several different jobs so that she could pay the bills." Ethan saw his father's eyes shining with unshed tears. "She didn't have anybody to help her, so the load was all on her. Where did you think the money came from to pay rent and buy groceries and clothes?"

"Well, she took in sewing. I know that because she sewed almost every night."

"She also did washing and ironing for folks, cleaned houses, made quilts and did crocheting to sell to tourists. She just did it all so graciously, that it seemed like nothing to you. And that's exactly the way she wanted it. But she was working, Son, all day every day. Working to earn money for you and for her."

"Still… that's not the same as Grace working at the newspaper. And Mom had no choice. Grace does."

James' voice softened. "I remember when you were a toddler. You ran your mother ragged every single day. She was exhausted all the time. I should have helped her more, but I was working at the sawmill every weekday, visiting the sick at night, working on my sermons on Saturday, trying to be a good pastor. She never complained, always supported me. Though she could get a little testy every once in a while, I remember. And who could blame her? She took care of the house and you and me, plus took in sewing even then. The sewing money was supposed to be your college fund…." James' voice broke.

"Hey." Ethan put his arm around James' shoulder. "I went to college, and everything worked out. God took care of all of us."

"I know." A comfortable silence ensued.

"Small children do take a considerable amount of time and energy. I admit I'm surprised that Grace thinks she can handle forty hours a week at the newspaper, plus have enough stamina to take care of a baby and the house."

"She wasn't planning to work forty hours."

"Twenty?"

"No. Twelve. Three mornings a week, four hours each."

"How long would she work those hours? Would she go back to full-time in the next year or so?"

"Well, no. Grace's plan is to work twelve hours a week until our children are in school. Then, she says, she plans to go to twenty hours a week. Later, when they're a lot older, maybe in high school, she might want to return to full time work."

"I see." For a moment, James pursed his lips in thought. "You know what I think, Son?"

"I think your wife is a wise and reasonable woman." Ethan's eyes opened wide as he stared in surprise at his father. "I think you should stop arguing about this, and understand that she has a God-given talent that she needs to use."

Ethan rose from the swing. "I'm surprised at you, Dad. I thought we would be in agreement on this. I know many in my congregation feel as I do."

"I'm sure they do."

The moment of tension was brief, and passed on.

Ethan's voice was back to normal when he said, "I'd better go find Grace now. She needs to get home and put her feet up for a while."

"Good idea. Let's go see if we can break up this hen party." Another burst of feminine giggles rolled out on the warm summer air. James said conspiratorially, "We may need reinforcements!"

Sixty-One

Saturday
September 5

Heaven's Mountain was beckoning him this morning. The sky was bright blue with small white clouds scudding across as if they had somewhere important to go, and the wind was blowing just enough to let him know that a change in the weather was coming soon. Before heading up the mountain, James stopped by the lawn and garden store to pick up a scythe and some lawnmower blades. Now that the house was basically finished, he needed to make his yard look presentable. It was a pleasant thought, that he had his own yard to work in again.

When he passed the Heaven's Mountain Church, he noticed the side door was open, so he turned his truck around and went back. That door was always left unlocked. Someone could have not shut it tight, he supposed. All seemed to be well until he went inside the church. There were several beer bottles scattered around the altar and one empty pint bottle of Jim Bean sitting on the pulpit. There was also a half full jar of pickled pigs feet under the front pew. Walking in a few more feet, he felt his shoe slide in something slick. He looked down. Tobacco juice! Now he could see that there were a number of wet spots.

Well, his yard work would have to wait just a little longer. There was a supply closet in the foyer and a water spigot outside. The only other thing needed was a little elbow grease.

An hour had passed by the time James got the church cleaned up, a slightly troubling, but still minor, inconvenience to his day. He was feeling mighty comfortable in his world today. No dreams in the last two nights, which he attributed to God helping him with his "homework" this week. The habits of thinking that way were still there, but he had faith that perseverance in rejecting those thoughts would succeed in time.

He closed the door tightly, walked around to his truck, and was about to get in when he saw a narrow plume of smoke a short distance away. His driveway was only a quarter mile down the road and in that same general direction, but he couldn't think of any reason for a fire to have started close to his property. Nevertheless, he jumped in and cranked the truck quickly.

By the time he was on the driveway, he knew it was either the house or one of his outbuildings. When he rounded the last curve and the wooded view opened up to reveal his yard, he could have cried – with relief! It was one of the larger, and better, sheds that was on fire, but he was so thankful it wasn't his house, he hardly cared. Nor did he care that the water hose came too late to do more than keep the fire from spreading.

So far, his morning had been spent cleaning the church and putting out a fire. What would be next? At any rate, all that physical exertion had made him thirsty. Since he now had a refrigerator here, he'd been keeping some soft drinks nice and cold so he would have one handy when he wanted to cool off. He got one and went to sit on the back porch for a few minutes.

He had drunk all but a swallow of the coke when he happened to look down the mountain towards Thelma's place. He saw smoke. He went to the bedroom to get the binoculars he'd been using lately to watch the wildlife.

Hurrying back to the porch, he adjusted the focus until he could see the details of their yard. He could see the flames now. It was the porch, which was screened in on three sides and attached to the house on the fourth side. The corner away from the house was burning strongly and the smoke was growing. He scanned the yard to see if any other structures were involved and that's when he saw Gus Woody, standing next to the tool shed, a red gas can in his hand.

What conceivable purpose could that scoundrel have for hurting those people? No matter. The sheriff could deal with Woody later. Right now, he needed to go put out another fire.

As he ran through the house, he wished he had gone ahead and had his phone installed. Grabbing his keys, he hopped back in the truck and spun it around, dust and gravel flying. His thoughts were racing, too. He remembered that Thelma and Billy were driving Katherine back to school and wouldn't be back until this afternoon. He decided he had a better chance of saving the house if he had help, so he whipped into the driveway right before Thelma's, praying that the Wagners would be at home.

They must have seen the smoke, too, because Mr. Wagner and his son were already in their station wagon, motioning for him to turn around.

The Wagners seemed to know where everything was located, the outside water spigot, the hoses, a second faucet by the garage. Soon there were two streams of water working on dousing the flames. The hardest part to get under control was the roof, where the fire was moving toward the other part of the house, past the screened in porch, but they finally got it so drenched that it seemed safe to turn off the water.

Mr. Wagner wiped the perspiration from his forehead. "They may have some damage in the kitchen, right next to the porch, but it's nothing like it could have been." He held out his hand to James, who shook it heartily. "Good job, Preacher. Want to join the Volunteer Fire Department?" he joked.

"You, too, Preston." James took hold of his shirt and fanned it in and out. The he remembered the culprit behind all this mess. "Hey, I saw Gus Woody through my binoculars – same time I spotted the fire down here. Have you seen him this morning?"

"No. You actually saw him here?"

"Right over there next to that tool shed. Had a red gas can in his hand, too."

"I always knew he was ignorant and mean, but what in the world would possess him to do such a thing?"

"I don't know, but my own tool shed burned down this morning. It was on fire when I got to the house a little while ago. I put it out, but lost the shed."

Preston's son Marty walked over. "Were you asking about Ole Gus?"

His father answered, "Yeah. You seen him today?"

"Well, yeah, at least I'm pretty sure it was him. Doesn't he drive an old beat-up Dodge truck? Maybe a '55 model. Used to be blue?"

"That's him," said James.

"He was pulling out of the church parking lot this morning when I drove by. Must have been about eight o'clock."

"That explains the beer bottles and tobacco juice I found in the church this morning," James remarked.

He and Preston exchanged glances, then Preston said, "I 'spect I better go check my place, and then, Preacher, maybe you and Marty should go talk to the sheriff. I'll call up the neighbors, let them know what's going on. I'll keep an eye on your house while you're gone, James."

Sixty-Two

Sunday
September 6

On Sunday morning, Mr. Reithoffer arrived in Fairmount in a foul mood. Out of some one hundred property owners, only eight had signed off on the options, and those were all properties of little value. During the past week, he had contacted most of the remaining owners, with little success. In fact, English, before his accident, had procured seven of the eight signatures, Reithoffer only one. This did not sit well with Mr. Reithoffer.

Tomorrow the cat would officially be out of the proverbial bag, one way or the other, so today would be his last chance to get the signatures he had promised to the corporate office. And, he decided, Mr. English, injured or not, was going to help him get them.

Unfortunately, Mr. English was not as cooperative as he had expected. "Sunday is not a good day to approach these people, Mr. Reithoffer. They attend church on Sunday morning, most of them. Some of them go on Sunday evening, too. They have family over for Sunday dinner. They're not going to respond well to your interruption."

"They'll just have to get over it. How soon can you be ready?"

"Ready for what?" asked Tom, though he was fairly certain of what was coming.

"You're going with me. You evidently commune with these mountain people better than I do, so you're coming, too."

Tom weighed his choices. If he went, he could ease the abrasive nature of Reithoffer's pitch. On the other hand, he no longer trusted his associate, or the company they worked for, and he really didn't want to risk his own reputation any longer by aligning himself with them.

"No. I'm not going with you."

Mr. Reithoffer seemed disgusted. "Yes, you are. I'm ordering you to go."

"No, Mr. Reithoffer, you are not. You may consider this verbal communication as my official resignation. I'll have a written confirmation in your hands later today, if you wouldn't mind stopping by to pick it up on your way out of town."

"You're a fool, English," said Reithoffer as he turned and strode haughtily out the door.

"Ah, but an honest fool," said Tom.

Sixty-Three

Monday
September 7

Shortly after ten o'clock on Monday morning, the story came over the AP wire into the offices of The Fairmount Chronicle:

The Public Service Commission announced this morning that construction will begin in June, 1971, on a new power plant and dam near the Coltrane Valley in north Georgia. Several locations were under consideration by the Planning Council, who arrived at their final decision only earlier today. Other proposed locations that were eliminated were Kirkatani Ridge and the Heaven's Mountain area.

That was all Grace was waiting for. Thanks to Ed, who had made a few phone calls to some of his friends who were "higher-ups" in the state government hierarchy, she had known on Saturday that the announcement was coming today. This gave her ample time to pull together all the background information on Stockton and tie it in to the dam construction. She had already written the article which described the company's push to obtain options on the land which would have surrounded the newly created lake, had Heaven's Mountain been selected as the site.

Joe should be on his way back from the beach right now, thought Grace. Hallelujah! She always thought she could handle most anything, but the last week would have been draining even if she hadn't been eight and a half months pregnant. Tomorrow, when Joe was in the office, she would get him up to speed, then she planned on writing the article about the arson episodes up on the mountain over the weekend. From James, she had already gotten an eye-witness report, and the Sheriff had agreed to an interview for late this afternoon, even though it was the Labor Day holiday. Apparently, Mr. Woody was still at large, but the evidence for his conviction appeared to be compelling. No motive yet, though. Strange.

All in all, she thought, quite a week for news in the little town of Fairmount.

Sixty-Four

*H*ard to believe it was the second week in September already, thought James. The leaves had barely begun to turn, but their dry rustle spoke of their imminent departure. He was standing on the back porch of the old Lucas place gazing out over the view of mountain ranges spread across the horizon. To think he could sit on his own back steps and see this anytime he wanted! It was more than he'd ever expected when he walked out of prison.

The property was in poor condition, barely livable, when Bo signed it over to him, but James saw the potential in the location and the bones of the structure and made the decision to eventually make it his home.

He walked away from the edge of the wide covered porch and pulled the squeaky screen door open. Right inside the door he stopped and took in a different sort of view. The dark wood floor shone with the recent re-finishing. To his left was the kitchen area, now modernized with new appliances, counter tops and cabinets. He had also added a wide counter to separate the kitchen from the living area. To the right, the dining table and chairs sat on a homemade rag rug given to him by Miss Sally.

Beyond the dividing counter was the living room, with the centerpiece being the original stone fireplace, flanked on each side by light forest green armchairs built by Jed Liles. James hadn't minded the slight extravagance, knowing that those chairs would stand the test of time, besides adding beauty to his home. When he could afford it, he would add a sofa, to sit a little further back, right in front of the fireplace.

The rooms were light and airy with the new larger windows he'd installed and James was pleased that they let in not only the light but also the beauty of the surrounding mountainside. Satisfied, he walked on through to the short hall.

First on the left was the original bathroom, which had been completely refurbished. At the end of the hall were two bedrooms, both a good size. James pushed open the door to the one on the right. This would be his room, with its own bath and with French doors opening on to the back porch and his own personal view. The attached bath was a completely new addition to the house but the extra work and expense would give him true privacy, a comfort he hadn't known in many years.

The repairs and renovations were basically complete now. There was no reason for him not to formally move in to his house and move out of his room at the boarding house. Because Gus Woody was still at large, posing a possible risk for more fires, he'd spent the last two nights here anyway. Might as well make it official.

Yes, it was time he had his own place.

Sixty-Five

Monday evening, just after dark, Mr. Reithoffer and Gus met in their usual spot in the park. Gus didn't wait for any pleasantries to be exchanged.

"I want my money now."

"You're only going to get half of what you expected. That's all there is."

"Oh, no, you don't. You're giving me all of it."

"The deal fell through. Didn't you hear it on the radio? The dam is going somewhere else, so all that mountain land is just that, mountain land, and not some prime lakeside realty."

Gus's eyes were narrow slits now. "That don't matter to me. I want my money. I did what you said. I made 'em see they were too far away to get any protection from fire and police and ambulance."

Reithoffer snorted. "No, you made a mess, that's what you did. You killed somebody's dogs, when what I wanted you to do was make them afraid of all the wild animals up here. Like bears and mountain lions. That's what you were supposed to kill, and just leave them out where they'd find them. And then you went and got caught setting those fires!"

"Yeah, I'm a wanted man for doing your business for you. Seems to me you owe me a whole lot more than you promised."

"You screwed up on everything you did! Are you just stupid or what?"

Gus had been fondling the knife in his pocket and when Reithoffer called him "stupid" he brought it out, ready to use it.

Reithoffer jumped back. "Ho! Hold it, I didn't mean anything!"

Gus was crazy mad now, screaming, "Where's my money?"

Looking all around to see if anyone could be hearing this ruckus, Reithoffer caved, pulling an envelope from his pocket. "Here. Here it is." Reaching into another pocket he extracted another stack of bills and handed it all to Gus. "All of it. Take it."

Greedily, Gus grabbed the cash. "I'm not gonna kill you. But if you ever rat me out, you can be sure it's comin'. Just like that holy-roller preacher that gave me away to the sheriff. His payback is comin' and it's comin' real soon."

Sixty-Six

Tuesday
September 8

"You missed it, Joe."

"Yeah, you shoulda been here." The Chronicle staff wasn't about to let him through the door without some big-time ribbing.

"I know, I know." Joe held up his hands in surrender. "Two big stories in one week. But you guys came through for me. You're the best! And to show my appreciation, tomorrow I'm taking everybody out to lunch."

As cheers broke out, Joe reached Grace's desk. He pointed down at her and smiled, then leaned over to give her a hug. "And here is the young lady who spearheaded these investigations – our own Grace MacEwen!"

"Thank you very much." She inclined her head in a gracious bow. "Now, I'd suggest that we retire to your office, Joe, so you can get the low-down on where we stand on everything. The paper goes to print tomorrow and we've got a heck of a lot of work left to do today."

Sixty-Seven

"Afternoon, James. Want some coffee?"

"Thanks, I wouldn't mind having a cup. How are you, Mitch?"

"Doing great. You're looking rather chipper today." He motioned toward the sitting area. "What's going on with you?"

"I did my homework."

"And?"

"You were right. I always believed, if and when I was released, that I would resume the life I had before going to prison. My brain knew that wasn't going to happen, but my heart dreamed of it."

Mitch nodded his understanding and waited for James to continue.

"I still want my old life back. I do want the life I had with Betty. It makes me angry that I'm never going to have the chance to do that."

"Who is suffering because of that anger?"

"Just me."

"That's right. Just you. And why should you suffer with it? You can probably guess what I want you to do with that anger."

"I'd say, give it to God."

"Bingo! But that's not all there is to it, as you well know. You've grieved over your old life and Betty for long enough. It's time to place that great big part of your life gently and with great love in your past. I want you to start thinking of it that way. Practice thinking of that life as part of your history, a wonderful chapter in your life, but a chapter that has ended."

"Homework?"

"Yes, sir. The kind that's good for you."

Sixty-Eight

The day was too long, but not nearly long enough. Grace felt swollen all over and generally miserable. She had a new twinge in her back, too, that had caused her to jump out of her chair a few times today, in an effort to walk it off.

At four-thirty, when she finished her last article, the one about the fires, she scooped up all of her work and walked it into Joe's office, placing it on the corner of the desk.

"Thanks, Grace. Let's see what you've got." He began to read:

> *Heaven's Mountain was ablaze last Saturday with several small fires, all of which are believed to have been set by the alleged perpetrator, local resident Gus Woody, a forty-eight year old white male, lately of 1679 Oak Terrace, Fairmount, Georgia. Though his motives are as yet unknown, a reliable witness places the alleged arsonist at one of the crime scenes.*
>
> *Around ten-thirty a.m. Saturday, from his home higher up the mountain, local pastor James MacEwen saw smoke coming from the residence of Thelma Canfield. Using binoculars, he then identified the suspect who was standing in the Canfield yard, gas can in hand.*

Due to the efforts of Pastor MacEwen, neighbor Preston Wagner and his son Marty, the fire was contained and damage was for the most part limited to the porch area of the home.
Earlier that morning, MacEwen had extinguished an outbuilding fire at his own home, which the Sheriff's office believes was set by the same arsonist. Also possibly related is a case of vandalism at Heaven's Mountain Church, which was discovered by Pastor MacEwen around nine a.m. Saturday morning.

"As always, excellent work, Grace." As he scanned the rest of the several articles Grace had laid on his desk, he continued to speak. "Your expose on the Stockton Corporation will almost certainly be picked up by the wires. I'd bet on it."

When he finished the last article, he looked up. "Grace? What's wrong?"

Sitting in the guest chair, chin resting on her fist, Grace's eyes were closed. As she opened them, she gave a little jump. "What? I'm sorry, what did you say?"

"Nothing much, except 'great job'. Grace, you look like you're about to fall out of that chair. Why don't you go home?" He came around and helped her up to a standing position. "You've been a very busy girl for the last two weeks. I should have called Ed myself to come and help you, though he could not have done any better than you did!" He opened the door to his office. "Go home and get some rest and don't worry about this paper. I've got it from here."

"Okay, boss." For once there was no argument forthcoming.

At her desk, she called Ethan. "Hey, sweetheart. Yes, we're all done..... I'm getting ready to go home. Could you pick something up for your dinner? I'm really tired and my back is hurting for some reason. I think I'll just go straight to bed when I get home....I love you, too."

Sixty-Nine

For four days James had hardly been seen at the boarding house. Now, on Tuesday evening, he was making a point of being there for dinner.

Nan was still doing most of the cooking because Clare was still on crutches, though she had become quite adept at inventing ingenious ways to circumvent that hindrance. When James entered the dining room, she was unloading condiments from the deep pockets of her apron.

"Well, look what the cat drug in!" she said. "James, we've missed seeing you around here."

"I've missed seeing you all, too," he replied. The tempting aromas of fried chicken, corn on the cob and butter beans rose from the laden table. "My stomach says it has missed being here, too!"

"Preacher, where you been?" asked an old gentleman boarder.

"I've been staying at my place on the mountain."

Nan came in with a big bowl of mashed potatoes. "You haven't had any more trouble, have you?"

"No. It's been quiet. No problems."

"And they haven't caught ole Woody yet. 'S'what I hear," said the old gentleman.

"Not yet," James confirmed.

As usual, the boarders seemed to know when supper was on the table. The rest of them all converged on the dining room within a few seconds of each other, greeting James with a pat on the back or a handshake.

Clare spoke loudly over the general din. "James, would you ask the blessing for us?" Quieting down, everyone joined hands around the table.

"Lord, your mercies toward us are incredible and generous beyond what we deserve. Your love is a gift that is life changing. Your provision for us is constant and fills all our needs. Thank you, Father, for the food that is now set before us. Bless the hands that have prepared this meal and bless us to serve you daily according to your will and purpose. In our Savior's name we pray. Amen."

James took note of the fact that Tom remained in his seat to Clare's left and that now, apparently due to his own extended absence, Nan was now ensconced in the chair on her right. It made perfect sense and he had no blame to place on anyone.

With a humble attitude he took a seat by the retired teacher and made an effort to be friendly while attempting to keep his wayward eyes from drifting too often to the end of the table. He noticed that Clare was not very talkative, but Tom and Nan maintained the conversation on their own.

When dinner was over and the cooks had been sufficiently complimented, everyone pitched in to get the table cleared and the dishes carried into the kitchen, while Clare gave instructions and made decisions, generally bossing everyone around in a joking, good-natured way.

Finally, there was no one left but Nan, Clare, Tom and James.

"Clare, I can tell you're drooping. Why won't you just relax and let us do this for you?" Nan fussed.

"You've already done so much..." protested Clare.

"Tom and I are going to clean up the kitchen tonight," Nan insisted. "James, get her out of here before she tumbles off those crutches."

"I'm not too tired..." said Clare, but seeing the look she was getting from Nan, she acquiesced. "But I'm going."

James took her by the upper arm and guided her away from the kitchen. "It's board game night anyway. Come on. I'll help you get things set up, and then I'd better get going."

In her quarters off the kitchen, she sat down in the armchair and threw a pillow on the ottoman to support her leg. "Do you have to go so soon? It's not dark yet. Can't you stay awhile longer?"

"Afraid not. Until they get Gus, I need to be there to watch the house." He picked up a couple of games. "What's it gonna be tonight? Scrabble? Rook?" He held them up for her consideration.

She ignored the games. "Can we just talk for a few minutes? Before you have to leave?"

She seemed pensive tonight, he thought. "Sure. I needed to talk with you anyway."

Seventy

"I thought you were asleep," said Ethan, as his wife came dragging into the kitchen, holding her hands over her eyes to shield them from the light.

"I can't get comfortable," she complained, coming behind his chair to put her arms around his neck. "Every time I drift off, my back wakes me up again." He patted her arm. Across the kitchen table, he had spread out the papers from Harry Carroll. He had been working on a list of pros and cons regarding accepting the job, but he began putting it away now.

"What are you working on?" she asked.

He didn't want to open the door for an argument tonight, especially when Grace was already tired and ill. "Just the Carroll stuff." He closed the folder. Pulling her around in front of him, he gathered her into his lap and began rubbing her shoulders and arms. She closed her eyes again. "I'm sorry you can't sleep. Can I do anything to help?"

"This is good, what you're doing right now," she murmured.

He continued to massage her shoulders. "You've had a pretty rough week, haven't you?"

"That's an understatement. If I'd known it would be this draining, I think I would have called Ed myself."

Ethan was thinking, how do you think you're going to handle working at the paper when you've been up half the night with a finicky baby? He was only thinking of her and her welfare and the welfare of their child.

But that wasn't true and he knew it. His concern over what people would say about the pastor's wife working had a lot to do with it, especially the reaction from a rather legalistic, and very vocal, segment of his congregation. And, to muddy the waters even further, there was the fact that he would like to be able to make a decision about the very flattering offer from Harry Carroll without having to take into consideration his wife's needs and desires. He had to admit it. He wanted her to put his career first in their married life, give him one hundred percent support, and willingly limit her role to that of wife, mother, homemaker and pastor's wife. Once he laid all those hidden motives and ugly truths out on the table, he felt ashamed. That was not at all the kind of husband he wanted to be.

He realized that Grace had fallen asleep. He could tell by how relaxed her body had become. He didn't think he could get her into bed without waking her, so he decided he would just hold her right there in his lap. A few minutes sleep was better than none at all. If necessary, he would hold her all night.

Seventy-One

When James said he needed to talk to her, Clare couldn't help it, her heart leaped with hope even though she knew it was unlikely he was going to declare his undying love for her. But when he turned from the game cabinet to face her, his expression effectively negated that remote possibility. He didn't have the look of a man who was about to speak of love.

Although he *had* seemed to be looking at her in a different way this evening. But maybe he was just feeling vulnerable because of the fires. "What did you want to talk to me about?"

He hesitated. "Well, I… My house is finished."

"Why, that's fantastic, James!" She rejoiced for her friend's good news. "After all your hard work, you've finally got it ready?"

"Yes, it's pretty much all done, except for a few minor touches, here and there."

Clare observed, "You don't seem very excited. If it were me, I'd be bouncing off the wall, shouting it from the rooftop."

"Yes, I guess you would," he said. "But you know that means I'll be leaving your house?"

She put her hand over her mouth, crestfallen. "Oh, yeah. I wasn't thinking."

"You've been such a gracious host, Clare. I truly appreciate your many kindnesses to me, especially right after the pardon, when I was living with Ethan. You were a good friend to me, when I didn't have that many friends."

The thought of rarely seeing James was too much to bear. She could feel the tears pooling in the corners of her eyes. Clare mustered a weak smile. "Who's going to help me cook breakfast now?"

He ducked his head. "Maybe you can get Tom…"

But his reply was drowned out when Nan interrupted, "What are we playing tonight?" Then realizing her rudeness, she said, "Oh, I'm sorry, James, were you speaking?"

"What? Oh, no, no." He rose and rubbed his hands together. "In fact, I need to go. Nan, Clare, dinner was delicious. I know I won't get to enjoy meals like that every night from now on."

At Nan's and Tom's puzzled looks, Clare explained, "James is moving out."

Before the others could comment, James said, "I'll have all my things out by noon tomorrow, Clare." He raised his hand in parting. "Got to run. Good night, Nan, Tom. Good night, Clare."

Seventy-Two

Another stitch of discomfort across her back woke Grace around three a.m. Changing positions to lie on her other side, she vaguely remembered Ethan guiding her back to bed earlier in the night. Now, she guessed she would be awake for the duration, for lately she had a hard time getting back to sleep. For a long time she tried, but when she realized it was a hopeless cause she turned back her covers, being careful that her movements would not wake Ethan, and went to sit in the living room.

All the television channels had signed off by this time and she certainly didn't want to watch the test pattern, so she laid down on the couch and pulled the crocheted afghan over her. It only took a couple of minutes for her to realize that she was now completely and totally awake. Foot!

She got back up and wandered through the house, ending up in the nursery. She hadn't spent a lot of time around babies in general, so the idea of being responsible for such a tiny life was pretty overwhelming. Thank goodness her mother would be able to stay for several weeks, just until she became adjusted to the routine.

What would it be like to hold him – or her? She touched her belly and rubbed gently. She hoped she would be as good a mother as her own mother had been.

Things were going to change dramatically in this house. For two years, she and Ethan had concentrated only on each other. Now there would be someone else to consider, another schedule to juggle, another line item on their budget. Or maybe several more line items!

She picked up a stuffed animal, a little white lamb, and sat down in the rocking chair. Holding the lamb like an infant, she began to rock.

Maybe she and Ethan would be over all their little disagreements by the time the baby arrived. She knew she had been unusually difficult to deal with these last few weeks, and that a lot of the blame for the discord that existed between them was hers. After all, he had tried several times to discuss things with her. She was the one who had refused to talk.

The thing was, she felt a little betrayed. She thought Ethan supported her career and her writing. It made her feel that he respected her talent and her equal worth as a person. She had expected his encouragement for returning to work, especially considering the very limited hours she suggested. So his negative response to even those limited hours, which she thought reflected her acceptance of the major portion of child-rearing duties, was truly a shock to her.

Therefore when he then brought out the Carroll offer, her stubborn streak took over. If he couldn't discuss her career with any sort of reasonableness, then she would not discuss his. Of course, she hadn't really thought these things through, but the feelings that they generated had more or less controlled her responses without any sort of analysis on her part.

With the same driving instinct that compelled her to get her nest in order for the baby, she felt a strong urge to get things right with Ethan, now, before the baby was born. Somehow, they needed to tear down all these defenses and have an honest discussion. She wanted to go wake him up right that very minute.

He might not appreciate that though.

For the first time in weeks, she had a clear picture of her own behavior and she was ashamed. Hormones or no hormones, she hadn't treated her husband as she should have. A little cleansing talk with God was in order and now was as good a time as any.

Seventy-Three

Wednesday
September 9

"Good morning, Joe," said Ethan, from his booth in the diner.

"Mornin', Ethan. How's Grace today?"

"She was aleep when I left the house and I certainly wasn't going to wake her up! She hasn't slept well for the last month, and I know she was awake for several hours last night."

"Boy howdy, I remember those days when my wife was pregnant. But you know, every pregnancy was different, just like all three of our boys are different. Some are easy, some are difficult."

"I guess we can't complain," Ethan commented. "She's healthy and so is the baby. I'm sure it would improve her disposition if she could get a full night's sleep though.

"You're not counting on Grace being able to catch up with her sleep *after* the baby is born, are you?" said Joe incredulously. "Unfortunately, neither of you are going to get a lot of sleep anytime in the near future."

Ethan answered unenthusiastically, "So I hear."

"I'll share what I've learned with you, Ethan. With the first baby (of course, that would be my son Jack), we were still living in Atlanta, and I was working as the vice reporter for the Journal and Constitution. Lots and lots of overtime. I didn't help much with the nighttime feedings. I slept through it all and she got almost no sleep at all. So, naturally, she was exhausted the whole first year. She and the baby were sick every time you turned around. They were miserable and so was I.

"When the second and third babies came along, we were living here in Fairmount, and we did a whole lot of things differently. We took turns, so both of us got enough sleep. She and the babies were healthy. They were happy and so was I.

"So, Ethan, I'm telling you what someone should have told me: Take good care of your wife and make absolutely sure she gets enough sleep."

Ethan filed that away in his mental file labeled "Advice for Post-Delivery". "I believe you, Joe. I've already seen what lack of sleep can do to a woman."

"Moving on to another subject..." Joe continued. "I'm glad I ran into you this morning. Ethan, I had no idea these past two weeks were going to be so demanding. I certainly never intended to put so much on Grace during this last month before the baby comes. If we had had our normally quiet week of news, she could have gotten by working half-days the whole time. Instead she was working overtime. In hindsight, I wish I'd called Ed myself, instead of leaving it up to her."

Ethan reassured him, "I'm sure she wouldn't have let you do that without protesting."

"No, she didn't want me to call him, so I didn't. But she looked so tired when she left yesterday. I was worried about her."

Ethan nodded. "She was pretty worn-out. Went straight to bed."

"Ethan, she is so good at what she does. I don't know if you're aware of it, but she could work for any newspaper, anywhere."

"Really?"

"Yeah, really. Ed says she's the best journalist for her age that he's ever come across."

"Wow. I knew she was good, but..."

"I'm thrilled to have her, but honestly, she's overqualified for our little operation."

"You mean, if we stay here, she'll never get to fully use her gifts?"

"Well, of course, there's a chance she could do free-lance for magazines, that sort of thing. And there's always other options for writers.

She could write books, fiction or non-, or she could go into editing. Or teaching. I bet Grace would make a wonderful teacher."

Ethan had stopped listening. He was trying to reconcile what Joe was saying about Grace's abilities with his own dismissal of her work as relatively unimportant. His own sense of importance was definitely taken down a notch or two.

"Ethan, did you hear what I said?"

"I'm sorry, Joe. What did you say?"

"I said for you to tell Grace not to worry about coming in today at all, but to join us for lunch if she feels up to it."

"I will. I'll tell her."

As Ethan was leaving the diner, Diggy was coming in. "Preacher, I'm glad I ran into you."

Ethan chuckled, "I'm very popular that way today. Everyone is glad they ran into me."

Diggy wasn't laughing. In fact he looked quite serious. "My breakfast can wait for a few minutes. Can I walk with you a minute, Ethan?"

"Sure, Diggy. I was going to walk to the post office." They fell into step together.

"Good enough."

"Was there something in particular you wanted to talk to me about?"

"Yessir," Diggy said. He swiped his nose with a cotton handkerchief before continuing. "Let's see how to say this."

Ethan's curiosity was piqued now. He waited for Diggy to proceed.

"I'm worried about Preacher James."

"Why is that?"

"Well, sir," Diggy said, rubbing his chin, "He like to ran out of the church during worship service Sunday a week ago."

"What do you mean?"

"You know, most the time church lets out around eleven, sometimes a few minutes later."

Ethan nodded.

"It was right at ten thirty-eight and the sermon was on Joseph. Preacher stopped in the middle of his talk, asked me to say the benediction, and while I was prayin', he bolted out the side door." Diggy looked a little sheepish as he admitted, "I know, 'cause I kinda had my eyes open while I was prayin'."

"Do you think he was sick?" Ethan questioned.

"I don't rightly know. Maybe."

"Strange that he hasn't said anything about it. He probably had an upset stomach or some such thing."

"I don't know. It didn't seem like it was his stomach bothering him. It seemed more like his head or his heart."

Seventy-Four

Ethan had offered to help his father get moved into the mountain house later, but after absorbing a super dose of warnings from Joe at breakfast, he decided he should swing by the parsonage and check on his expectant and tired wife. She was not in the kitchen and the house was quiet. He tiptoed to their bedroom and peeked in. She was still in the bed.

"I'm awake," she said softly, without turning over to look at him. "I was just about to get up. Just five more minutes." He went to sit on the edge of the bed. A strand of hair was looped across her face; he laid it back in place.

"You don't have to get up at all if you don't want to. You need to rest, Grace."

"I don't have to get up?"

"No. Absolutely not. Joe's back now, and you don't have to go back to work at all unless you want to."

Grace cradled her belly as she changed positions to lie on her back. "I do want to work, Ethan, but I don't want to allow myself to overdo it," she grimaced, "like I have this week."

"Good idea. You get a little crabby when you're exhausted," he teased. She punched him in the arm playfully.

"Ethan, after our baby gets here, I don't want to go back to work full-time, but I have this drive within me, and I…"

"Shhh….." He placed a finger over her lips. "I'm sorry I've been so stubborn about it. You should write. God gave you that talent to use. I was wrong for not listening to you."

"Come and lay beside me for a minute, Ethan."

"I'm already dressed, Grace," he protested.

"What difference will a few wrinkles make? Please? Snuggle against me and feel the baby. He – or she – won't be in here much longer."

Giving in, Ethan crawled up on the bed and Grace turned back on her side, facing away from him. She took his hand and placed it with hers across her belly. The baby was rather still, only a few rolling movements, but enough to let Mom and Dad know all was well.

"Ethan?"

"Hmmm?"

"Since this seems to be a time for confessions, I have to apologize to you, also."

"For…?"

"For being hardheaded myself and not talking to you about the position with Harry Carroll. I will support you whatever you decide. I trust your judgment and I trust that you're going to follow the Holy Spirit's leading."

"Thank you, Grace. Especially because we both know, if I take the job, it will mean some extra burdens and sacrifices for you."

She pulled his arm tight around her. "It will all work out, baby."

Seventy-Five

"With your truck and my car, we ought to be able to make it in one trip, don't you think?" guessed Ethan.

"Maybe."

They walked together to Ethan's storage building. "I guess you'll be glad to have your storage shed back," commented James.

"It's not a big deal." Ethan opened the double doors. "Except for the chiffarobe in the very back, all your boxes and furniture are on the left. Ours are on the right."

James surveyed the stacks of boxes. "I didn't remember having this much." He turned around to look at Ethan. "It may take two trips. The chiffarobe, the roll-top desk, cedar chest, tables, and all these boxes."

"Now that I look at it again, you may be right, Dad."

"I still can't believe your mother, and then you, kept all these things for me for all these years."

Ethan shrugged. "You may not even want to keep all of it, but you can take your time looking through it now that you have your own home."

James knelt down and clicked open a metal footlocker, looked inside, then shut it. "I should have gone through it when I was released." He looked up at Ethan. "I just couldn't handle it then."

Ethan came to his father's defense. "Who could blame you, Dad?" To hear his father speak of not being able to handle something was a new experience for Ethan. He always seemed so calm, so confident, full of hope and trust. Perhaps, after all, his father was only human and sometimes needed to lean on his son, instead of things always being the other way around.

He had opened his mouth to ask about the Sunday episode that Diggy had mentioned, but James was already maneuvering the roll-top desk into the middle of the aisle. "Let's get the biggest pieces this trip," he suggested.

In the back of the pickup, they were able to fit the desk, the chiffarobe, and the cedar chest, plus some of the smaller boxes tucked around the sides. After filling the car and the passenger seat of the truck, they headed slowly up the mountain.

The desk went against the living room wall opposite the fireplace, the chiffarobe in the guest bedroom and the cedar chest at the foot of James' bed. The rest of the things were stacked up in the guest room for James to sort out later.

With the second trip they were able to get the rest, except for the clothes and personal belongings from the boarding house, which James would pick up on the next trip. By the time all of the second load had been carried in, the midday heat was upon them and the men had worked up a sweat.

"How 'bout some Pork'N'Beans and Vienna sausage for lunch? And an ice cold Coca Cola ? You can be my first dinner guest in my new home," James joked.

"Sounds good to me."

James had installed an antique Coke bottle opener on the wall by the back door. He popped open two of the icy drinks and handed one to Ethan.

"You want to eat on the back porch? There might be a little bit of a breeze out there. I've even got a table out there now."

"Can I carry something?" asked Ethan.

"Yeah, you take the cans," said James, pulling the canned goods from his freshly stocked pantry, "and I'll bring the can opener and some forks and napkins."

After saying grace, they talked about the few things James had left to do on the house, and they debated how soon the baby might come. It was during one of the lulls in the conversation that Ethan broached the subject of Diggy's concern.

"Dad, I was talking to Diggy this morning, and he's pretty concerned about you. Do you remember leaving the worship service – abruptly – two Sundays ago?"

"Yes. I do. I'm actually surprised no one has 'told on me' sooner."

"It wasn't that way, Dad."

"I know, I'm just teasing." He ran his hand through his hair. "I guess you could call it a panic attack."

Ethan was bemused. "A panic attack? You? Why?"

"I don't fully understand it myself yet, but I'm trying to figure it all out. I'm seeing a counselor in Gainesville – a very capable Christian fellow Martin recommended to me – and I believe I'm making progress."

This was hard to comprehend. "I'm still trying to understand. How long has this been going on?"

"The counseling? Just a couple of weeks."

"No. The panic attacks."

"They started almost right after I got out, two years ago. But the episodes were very infrequent at first, didn't seem like anything to worry about. Lately, the last few months, it's been a lot worse."

Ethan was hurt. "Well, how could I have not known? Why haven't you said anything to me?"

James shrugged. "Every time I started to tell you, it seemed like it was a bad time to bring it up. You've had a lot of things to deal with yourself in the past couple of months. Grace. A new baby on the way. Harry Carroll. I didn't want to put another burden on you, Son."

"Never, Dad. Never a burden. So, what is causing these attacks? Can it be resolved?"

"We're still working on that. Me, the counselor and God."

Seventy-Six

Thursday
September 10

"Mitch, there's one other area of my life that's giving me some difficulty."

"Go ahead."

"Over the last couple of years I've become good friends with a woman – my landlord, as a matter of fact." James paused.

"And why is that a problem?" asked Mitch.

"It's not. I think I'm the problem."

"Elaborate, please."

"Okay. Let me tell you about Clare. She's merry and lively, loves to laugh and have fun. She's got a huge heart for people. Her faith is strong and she lives it."

"Sounds like a wonderful friend."

"She is. The problem is, I think I may have fallen in love with her, without even knowing it was happening."

"That doesn't have to be a problem."

"Well, I think I may have missed the boat. She very bravely let me know she was interested a month or so ago. Actually, I had a panic attack when she told me." James shook his head at himself. "So, I didn't even answer her. It was rude, but at that moment I literally couldn't speak. And then it was too late."

"Why? You can just go talk to her now."

"No, I can't. Right after that, she met someone else. I can't disturb her happiness. Besides, there's something else keeping me away from her. Clare is an exceptional woman and she deserves someone who is worthy of her. Tom is smart, articulate, handsome, apparently wealthy, and he's lived a life filled with travel and the finer things in life. I've been in prison most of my life. Even though I committed no crime, I've been exposed to a side of mankind that is harsh and cruel and weak and unworthy. You can't completely erase the effects of that exposure or the strangeness of outside life after being behind bars for so many years. I'm way behind in many areas, and I don't think I'll ever catch up."

"Oh, James, my friend, you're awfully hard on yourself. If she cared about you so much that she was willing to risk the embarrassment of rejection, believe me, she has not forgotten all about you in a month. And if she's known you for two years, she knows you pretty well by now. Well enough to know what kind of man you are, prison or not. Go to her. Tell her how you feel."

"I can't," he said sadly. "She's with Tom now."

Seventy-Seven

All the way home, James considered the proposition set forth by Mitch. Was it true? Should he lay his feelings right out in the open and willingly accept the risk of rejection? Or even worse, the possibility of hurting Clare?

Less than three weeks ago, she had expressed her interest in being more than friends, and much to his regret, he had given her no response. Did she still wonder why?

And would Clare have given up on him so quickly? That didn't make sense, knowing what a spunky, assertive character she was. Just like her honest declaration to him, she was not one to shrink away from saying what needed to be said.

But there was Tom. An impressive gentleman, all around. In quick fashion, Clare seemed to have found solace in him. Or had she?

If there was even the remotest chance that Clare still had feelings for him, shouldn't he search out that truth?

At that point in his pondering, he was almost home, about to pass Heaven's Mountain Church. He jerked the wheel to pull into the church drive and turned full circle to head back down the mountain, to Fairmount and to Clare.

The closer he got, the more excited and hopeful he became. All the reasons to pursue this course grew stronger in his mind: Mitch thought he should do this. Clare had already made the first move, so she must have been attracted to him, just as he was, imperfections and all. And it wouldn't be like Clare to give up on something so quickly.

They had become good friends, close friends, and they knew each other's personalities well enough to know if the potential for something more existed. All of those reasons were convincing.

The boarding house came into view, and he quite oddly felt an affection for the old sprawling white sided home. Many good memories were associated with this house, and with Clare. Not having an abundance of the kind of normal happy times to remember in his adult life, those memories were especially precious to him.

His usual parking spot in the back yard was available. He stopped the truck, took a deep breath, and pulled open the handle. The back door to the kitchen was generally open, and Clare had always invited him to feel free to use it, so in spite of the fact that he was no longer an official boarder, he was comfortable opening the screen door and walking in. She was not in the kitchen. "Clare?" he called, waiting, but not hearing an answer.

He headed down the hall toward the living room area, stopping at the stairs to call again. "Clare?" She ought to be here, he thought. Her car is in the garage. In the foyer, between the dining room and the living room, he paused, looking to each side.

On the far side of the living room was the sunroom, with a bank of windows between the two rooms. The door was shut, cutting off most of the sound. Tom and Clare were sitting at the table, facing away from the living room. He saw Clare reach up and touch Tom's arm, in what could only be interpreted as an intimate manner. Then Tom must have said something funny, for Clare was laughing, shaking her head at Tom, as if to say, "you're such a funny guy". James could practically hear her infectious laugh in her head.

He loved that laugh.

Mountain Girl

He loved the woman to whom it belonged, too, enough to leave her alone in her happiness. Enough to walk away and never say all the things that were in his heart.

Seventy-Eight

Friday
September 11

"Really, Nan! I can handle it from here," insisted Clare, giving her friend a gentle shove toward her chair in the dining room.

"But, your leg...."

"My leg is not bothering me at all. Please, go sit down and eat." Clare was standing on her own, without the crutches, being careful to avoid putting much weight on the injured leg.

"See?" She demonstrated, using the crutches to move to the other side of the dining room, then putting them to the side so she could have full use of her arms. "You've been doing my work for two weeks. It's time for me to get back on board."

"Are you sure?" Nan hesitated, with her hand on the back of the chair.

From his seat directly across from her, Tom offered his opinion. "I think she means it."

"All right, then! That's settled." Satisfied, Clare "crutched" back into the kitchen. From the kitchen side, she still had a clear view of the dining room through the pass-through counter opening. She fixed herself a cup of coffee and returned to lean against the counter, just out of sight. She could hear Tom and Nan clearly.

Tom was saying, "I actually grew up in a smallish town in upstate New York. I was in the tenth grade when we moved to the city."

Nan answered, "I can't imagine living in a place like New York City. So many people! Didn't you ever feel like they were pressing in on you?"

"No, no, it isn't like that at all. It's different, of course, but there are so many advantages to city life. Opportunities of all kinds, culture, the arts. But, I do have to say, being here in Fairmount has reminded me how lovely and intimate small town life can be. It's something I'd like to experience again."

"Will you go back as soon as the doctor clears you?"

"I saw Dr. Teal yesterday as a matter of fact, and he said I was free to travel."

"Oh." The disappointment was evident in her voice. "When are you leaving?"

"I'll be here until a week from Saturday."

Nan perked up. "Another week?"

"Yes, I have some 'unfinished business', I guess you'd say. For one thing, I need to visit Mr. Liles at his furniture shop. Today, if possible. Would you care to accompany me?"

"Oh, no, I'm sure I shouldn't. Clare may need my help. And I really should spend some time with Grace."

"Well." Tom readied his plate to carry to the pass-through. "If you change your mind, I would be grateful for your company."

"I'm sorry I can't go." She sounded disappointed.

"Have a wonderful day," he said cheerfully, then placed his things on the counter and waved goodbye to the few stragglers left at the table.

Nan came straight into the kitchen, where Clare was lying in wait for her. Her first words were, "Why didn't you accept his offer?"

Nan was flustered by the abrupt question. "Oh, I couldn't!" she stammered.

"And why not?" Clare demanded.

"He was just being nice," Nan explained.

Clare struck a pose. "No, he wasn't. He wouldn't have asked if he hadn't wanted you to go."

Nan was unconvinced. "But why would he want *me* to go with him?"

At that Clare huffed, "Uh! You're kidding, right? Nan, you have the looks of a thirty-five year old, plus you're a natural at graciousness and culture."

Nan protested, "No more than you!"

"Oh, please. I'm just a simple old mountain girl. Anyway the point is, he asked you because he likes you, Nan. I've been watching the two of you." Clare got serious. "I think he's really attracted to you. What could it hurt to go with him today?" Clare could see in her friend's eyes that Nan was starting to relent a little.

"Don't you need me to help you?" asked Nan.

"Nope. I've got it covered."

"You're sure?"

"Yes, I'm positive. Now go. Catch up with him and tell him you've changed your mind."

Shaking her head, Nan obediently turned to leave.

Clare added, "Then go spruce up a little."

Nan cut her eyes toward Clare, eyebrows raised.

Clare decided to "pick" a little more. "Hey, if you didn't bring any appropriate clothes, you can go filch something from my closet. You can probably squeeze into it."

Nan walked away clucking, "Clare, Clare, Clare. I hope you don't need to borrow something of mine anytime soon."

Ethan sat down on the edge of the bed and gently shook his wife's shoulder. "Honey? You said for me to wake you before I left."

"Mmmmf. Phooey. Is is that late already? I don't want to get up yet."

"Couldn't sleep? Is it still your back?"

"Yes! Every hour or so it woke me up." Grace sat up and rubbed her eyes. "I'm okay. It's not hurting now." She smiled sleepily and put her arms around Ethan. "The ladies at the paper want to take me out to lunch. I hate to disappoint them."

"By the way, Nan called a few minutes ago, just to check on you. She said she'd call back later."

"Thanks. I'll call her when I get to the paper."

Clare was just finishing up the breakfast dishes when Nan came down the back stairway which led directly from the third floor into the kitchen. She stopped at the bottom and stood ready for inspection. "How do I look?"

Clare dried her hands and gave her full attention. Nan had chosen a simple yellow Villager shirtdress, cinched at the waist by a John Romaine alligator belt, and gold Pappagallo flats. A matching lightweight cardigan with pearl buttons made the outfit sophisticated without being fussy.

"Perfect," pronounced Clare, walking over and giving Nan a hug. "You look great!"

Nan held Clare's hands and said, "One more thing. Are you absolutely certain you have no romantic interest or ties to Tom? Because if you do…"

Clare was emphatic. "No romance between Tom and me, I promise. Only friendship." She smiled conspiratorially. "But I believe I see something else in his eyes when he looks at you."

To which an embarrassed Nan responded, "Oh, hush!"

Seventy-Nine

Tom had replaced his wrecked red Camaro with a new one, black this time, with red leather interior. He had also changed his style of driving, now approaching the mountain area's tricky curves with caution.

Though she had felt a little intimidated initially, Nan was enjoying the feeling of being "courted", if that's what this was. And if it wasn't, well, she was still enjoying the feeling and the outing.

As they pulled into the parking area, Tom asked, "Can I take you into my confidence?"

Intrigued and flattered, she answered, "Yes, of course."

"You will be hearing of this when we enter the shop. I thought it best to explain the situation myself, before we go in. I am presently in negotiations with Mr. Liles, to form a partnership with him."

"A partnership? Are you going to build furniture, too?"

"Probably not, although I might try my hand at it eventually. Right now, I am going to infuse some capital into the business so that he can hire some skilled craftsmen to assist him. And I'm going to market his products, first to New York and then… who knows?"

"How exciting!" Nan clapped her hands together. "What made you think of doing this?"

Tom warmed to his subject. "To start with, his work is exquisite. And then, my sister's reaction to the pictures I sent her confirmed my own instincts." Getting out of the car, he came around to open her door. "Plus, I like the idea of settling down in this area, while still maintaining a strong attachment to New York."

"Best of both worlds," she commented.

"Precisely."

Eighty

After an uncomfortable night, Grace was very grateful that the back pain seemed to have eased off. Things were back to their normal quiet state at the offices of The Fairmount Chronicle, so much so that, Grace realized, it wasn't really necessary for her to be there at all. She piddled away the morning writing a couple of local interest pieces and proofreading copy. It was not very challenging, not like last week's whirlwind of activity. In spite of her adamant insistence to continue working until her due date, the combination of sleeplessness and intellectual boredom had her seeking out her boss. "Joe? Got a minute?"

"Sure, Grace. What's up?"

"It seems like everything is running smoothly this week, so…. I think I'm going to stay home from now until the baby comes. Do you mind?"

Joe smiled indulgently. "No, not at all. In fact, it's kind of a relief, because I've been worried you were trying to do too much."

"Well, I am really tired. I guess last week is catching up with me. But I am coming back part-time eventually, so don't give my spot away," she warned him.

"No need to worry about that," he said.

Margaret stuck her head in the door. "We're ready whenever you are, Grace."

"Go on," said Joe. "You ladies have fun."

As the four of them were going out the door, Margaret said, "Let's go to the new Tea Room. Would that suit you, Grace?"

"Sounds great. They have wonderful chicken salad."

"Oh, and those cute little cucumber sandwiches – to die for," said Patty.

A short walk later, and they were being seated by the hostess. As they waited for their server, Patty asked, "Have you decided what to name the baby?"

"Well, if it's a girl, we've decided to name her…Ohhhhh!!" The back pain had returned, and with a vengeance. Grace gasped as the pain sharpened and seemed to spread.

The women reacted quickly with concern. "What is it?" "Are you in labor?" "What can we do?" "Do you want me to call Ethan?"

Finally, it began easing and she was able to reply, "It's my back. It's been hurting off and on for the last couple of days."

"Comes and goes?" asked Margaret. "Show me where."

Grace placed her hand on her lower back. "Yes. It's passed now. I don't know what I did to pull those muscles!"

The older woman took hold of Grace's arm and grinned. "Sweetie, you're in labor. That's how my labor pains were at the beginning, right across my lower back."

Grace's hand flew to her mouth. "Oh, good grief!" Her eyes were huge as she looked around the table at her friends. "I feel so stupid."

"Is that the only pain you've had this morning?" asked Margaret.

"Unh-huh. It woke me up several times last night, but then it eased off early this morning and I haven't had any more pain until just now."

"Well, when the pains start coming closer together, you'd better high-tail it to the hospital. Don't dilly-dally either."

"Maybe I should go home. Or call Ethan," she worried.

Margaret brushed her concerns away. "No need rushing to the hospital until you have to. You're fine unless the pains come faster." The waitress had finally appeared, order pad ready. "Grace, what would you like, dear?"

Grace ordered the chicken salad plate, but she wasn't there to eat it when the waitress brought the food. The cozy little tea room was quite busy that day, so the ladies were still waiting when Grace experienced another labor pain only nine minutes after the earlier one. When another contraction followed on its heels even the intrepid Margaret agreed that Ethan needed to be called.

Grace followed the waitress to the back and made the call. "Ethan?"

"Well, hi. I thought you were having lunch with the ladies."

"I am. I was, but…." She paused. "It's time!"

It took him a second or two to digest that information. Then he responded, "For the baby?"

"Yes!! Come and get me!" Grace was excited now. "We're at the new tea room."

"I'll be right there."

And he was. Grace had barely made it back to her seat and updated her coworkers on her status, when Ethan came barreling through the door. Scanning the diners and zeroing in on her location, he hurried over and knelt by her chair. His voice full of concern, he asked, "Are you all right?"

"I'm fine, but we need to go. I've had three contractions in a row!"

"Okay." Ethan seemed to be at loss. "Okay then. Can you walk?"

The older ladies at the table exchanged amused looks. Grace simply slipped on her shoulder bag and stood up. "Honey, I'm fine," she reassured her husband, then to her coworkers, "I'm sorry I can't stay for lunch! We'll let you know when we have some news." Ethan put his arm around her for support and they made their way to the door. The diner's patrons, who had suspended their meals to watch the goings-on, began to clap and whistle and shout good wishes. Ethan just grinned and waved at them as the door closed behind them.

With Grace safely settled in the passenger seat and Ethan behind the wheel again, he asked, "Do we have time to go by the house and pick up your suitcase?"

Grace bit her bottom lip. "I don't really know. I think so…? I've not done this before, Ethan." She leaned back in the seat and took a deep breath. "Yes. Yes, we have time." She reached over and patted his hand. "Let's go to the house first."

As they pulled into their drive, Grace took charge. "I'll call your dad and my mom. You go get my overnight bag – it's in the closet, all ready to go. And don't forget my make-up bag on the counter in the bathroom."

Meantime Ethan was running around to her side, opening the car door and helping her out. She added, "Get the baby journal book, too. You know, the one Ed gave us. I want to write it all down while it's fresh on my mind."

She called her mom first. Clare answered the phone. "She's not here right now. She and Tom rode over to Liles Furniture shop. They ought to be back any time now."

"Oh, good," Grace said with relief. "Clare, tell her it's time! We're on our way to the hospital right now."

"Ohhhh, Grace! You're doing okay, right?"

"I'm great," she said, but she could feel the faint twinge of a contraction coming on. "Will you make sure Mom gets the message, Clare?"

"Absolutely. The minute she gets here. Oh, her car is in the shop, remember? But don't worry, she can use my car."

Grace took in a sharp breath as the pain escalated. "James isn't there, is he?"

"No, but I heard him say he was going to replace a door for Mrs. Strickland this morning. Do you want me to track him down for you?"

Grace managed a brief answer. "Yes, please. Got to go. Thanks, Clare."

Ethan was taking his sweet time, she thought, as the pain peaked and began to subside. "Ethan, come on," she yelled.

"I'm coming," he answered. She could hear him coming down the hall now. Around the corner he came, with her bag, her makeup case, the journal, and another overnight bag. "Decided I'd better grab some things, too, since we might be waiting through the night."

"Good thinking!" she complimented him. "But we'd better go now. I just had another contraction."

Back in the car, Grace wondered what her mother was doing at the furniture shop with Mr. English. That scenario seemed a little strange. She had no time to ponder on it, though, for there were too many other pressing issues to consider at the moment. One of which was the fact that she had forgotten to call her doctor to let him know she was on the way to the hospital. Ethan was putting the key in the ignition when she stopped him. "Ethan, go back in and call the doctor. The number is on the pad right by the phone."

"Right." He immediately made haste to do her bidding.

Eighty-One

Mission accomplished, Ethan relocked the back door and hurried to the car. They had spent more time at the house than he had anticipated and he was beginning to feel anxious about reaching the hospital before Grace reached a critical state. He could deliver a sermon, but not a baby!

"All right, sweetheart. The doctor said he'd meet us there." Ethan backed out of the driveway. Finally, they were on their way. He glanced down at the gauges, and felt his heart drop. The gas was almost on empty! Then he remembered. He had meant to fill up when he got back from criss-crossing the county with some of the youth group yesterday afternoon. How could he have forgotten? Wally's words popped into his mind, accusing him.

"Uh, Grace?"

"Yes, dear?"

"I'm sorry, hon, but it's going to be a few more minutes before we can start towards Gainesville. I've got to stop at Wally's to get gas."

When Grace turned to look at him, it was obvious she was having trouble understanding how he could have let this happen. But as he watched, he witnessed the irritation in her eyes giving way to mercy and love. She rubbed his arm and reassured him. "That's okay, baby. Let's go get some gas." Never had he been more thankful for the sweet disposition of his wife.

Even Wally took pity on him, or else he could tell by the expression on Ethan's face that now was not the time to say "I told you so". Wally got the car serviced about as fast as humanly possible, and Ethan wasted no time pulling back onto the road as soon as the gas cap was back on. He didn't even hear Wally saying, "Ethan, you forgot to pay," because at that moment, Ethan was watching his wife tough it out through another labor pain.

When it was over, she laid her head back against the seat as she rubbed her belly. "That one was different," she commented. "It wasn't just my back. I could feel it all across the front, too."

"Are you all right?"

She popped up and leaned over to put her arms around him, kissing him on the cheek, then singing out, "We're going to have a ba-by!" She scooted back over to her side. "I'm great! And I'm so excited!"

Mystified by her ability to put aside any concerns she might have, and her physical pain, and just enjoy the moment, he decided she had made the better choice and though he was still going to keep his feet firmly on the ground, he wasn't going to miss sharing this moment of joy with his mate.

He reached for her hand and squeezed. "So am I. I'm excited, too," and then he sang, in his slightly off-key way, "'Cause we're going to have a ba-by!"

It was worth the effort, for the look she gave him was pure adoration.

Eighty-Two

When Mrs. Strickland called him into the house to take the phone call, James had her front door laid across two sawhorses and was in the midst of replacing one of the panels. He wiped his feet carefully before entering the widow's immaculate house and was careful not to touch anything but the phone.

"James? It's Clare."

"Hello, Clare," he answered, wondering why she was calling him.

"Grace and Ethan are on the way to the hospital!" she cried with excitement.

"They are?" he said, his enthusiasm matching hers. "Gosh, I've got at least another hour to finish up here – can't leave until the door is back on its hinges – and then I need to get cleaned up a little…."

"You've probably got plenty of time," she assured him. "First babies usually take their time."

He asked before thinking, "Will you be coming to the hospital?"

"Not today, I can't get away. I'll pop over in the morning," said Clare. "You go on now, finish up and get yourself to the hospital. This grandbaby of yours is going to want to meet its grandpa."

That thought was so wonderful, it brought tears to his eyes.

Clare had expected Nan and Tom to be back long before lunch, so after the call from Grace, she called Jed Liles at his shop. According to him, Tom had been asking about a good place to eat lunch in Gainesville, and his best guess was that they had driven over there to eat lunch.

Considering Nan's initial reluctance to even accept the invitation, Clare had to admire the woman's gumption in staying the course for lunch, too. Things must be going very well indeed between the two of them, she thought. However, Nan could have picked a better day to have herself a fling! How was she supposed to get in touch with them in Gainesville? Then, she thought of "Little Lester" Lomax, a former boarder of hers who had also been a member of Fairmount Community Church, Ethan's church. Little Les, whose nickname belied his behemoth size, now worked for the Gainesville Police Department as a uniformed traffic officer. Bingo!

Nan had the scrumptious bite of chocolate cake on her fork, poised just at her lips, when the policeman appeared, an overmuscled colossus standing at attention beside their table.

"Excuse me, sir," said he, in a deep booming voice. "Is that your black Camaro parked out front?"

Tom nodded. "Yes, sir, officer. Is there a problem?"

The stiff giant turned into a teddy bear, shuffling his feet awkwardly. "Gosh, no. Miss Clare asked me to find you two, is all! She wanted me to tell this lady that her daughter and Preacher Ethan are on their way to the hospital right now!"

Nan threw the fork down, scattering chocolate crumbs across the white tablecloth. "Oh! Oh, my goodness!" Her eyes flew to the gentleman sitting across from her. "Tom, can you take me to the hospital?"

"Why, I'd be absolutely delighted!"

Eighty-Three

Three hours later James arrived at the maternity waiting room to find that Nan was already there, and for some reason, so was Tom.

"Have you been here long?" James asked.

"About an hour," replied Nan. "Ethan came out a little while ago. He said everything is going well, the doctor will be down here soon, and then I can go to the room and stay with her for a while."

"I guess there's no way of knowing how long it might be?"

"No. Not yet."

They sat down and chatted for a while. When Nan mentioned that the alternator had gone out on her car again, James realized that Tom must have given her a ride due to her own car being out of commission. Since Nan was probably going to be otherwise occupied now, first with Grace and then with the new baby, Clare might be counting on Tom's help at the boarding house.

"Tom, if you need to get back to the boarding house, I'll be glad to give Nan a ride whenever she needs it," James offered.

"That's very kind of you, but I'll stay. I don't mind at all."

James nodded in acceptance, though he was puzzled, to say the least. Shouldn't Tom be back in Fairmount helping Clare, who was still on crutches?

A few minutes later Ethan, looking quite the anxious expectant father in his pea-green scrubs, bustled in to the room. He hugged his father as everyone crowded around for the latest report.

"Everything is great, the doctor says. She's not even close to fully dilated yet, though, so it's going to be a while. He said it could be a few hours or it could be another whole day. I hate for you all to have to sit here in this waiting room that long. You could go home and come back later if you want."

"I'm not going anywhere, Son," James assured him.

"Neither am I," said Nan. Then a little impatiently, "Can I go back there now?"

"Sure, Mom. She's in room 216. You can stay with her from now on, as long as you want."

Nan gave a little wave and hurried out, her mind clearly focused on her daughter.

For a few more minutes, Ethan stayed and talked, but then he, too, left to return to his wife's side. The only ones remaining in the waiting room were James and Tom. They both made attempts to initiate and maintain a conversation, but couldn't seem to sustain any discussion longer than a few minutes. Every few hours Ethan and Nan made brief appearances but with no significant progress to report. Around eleven p.m., James made another offer to relieve Tom of his role as chauffeur, but Tom declined his offer.

It was a long night.

Eighty-Four

A little before nine p.m., Clare was done with all of her chores for the evening. The dinner dishes had been washed and put away, breakfast preparations had been made, and her customary final inspection of the communal living areas was completed. Of course, these evening rituals were generally dispatched with much more efficiency, but dealing with crutches cost dearly of her time.

Earlier that evening, she had called the hospital and talked to Grace and to Nan. She wished she could be there with her dear friends, but once again, here she was, tied down with her seemingly never-ending responsibilities at the boarding house.

She caught herself before the full descent into self-pity. There was so much for which she should be thankful, she reminded herself.

With the boarding house her aunt had so generously left to her, she was decently comfortable and secure, unlike many women of her age who, like her, had no specialized training or education. Sure, it was tons of hard work, but she was her own boss and she felt a fair amount of pride in the excellence of the accommodations she provided.

And friends. She was blessed to have so many true friends. Just look at how they had rallied 'round her these last few weeks, stepping in to help wherever needed.

But it was very lonely sometimes, and for some reason tonight the isolation was hitting hard. She loaded up the turntable with her favorite LP's, and made herself comfortable on the couch, her leg propped up on soft pillows.

The record on the bottom of the stack plopped down and the needle shushed across the plastic. Elvis. "Are You Lonesome Tonight". Boy, could she pick 'em!

Regardless, she lay there with her eyes closed and let the strains of his voice and the guitar wash over her. Somehow it was fitting. "Tell me, dear, are you lonesome tonight?" his dulcet voice asked.

Yes. Yes, she was lonesome. It seemed as if she had been lonesome forever. She ached sometimes for someone to hold her. She yearned for someone to whom she could tell the little stories of the day. She had thought that someone might be James, but maybe it was time to let go of that little dream of hers.

The song ended. Clare sighed. She adjusted her mindset, willing it back to a good place. She had never been one to feel sorry for herself and she wasn't going to start now. God had blessed her with a merry heart, not just for her own benefit but to heal and bless others, and by golly, she was going to hang on to that blessing and spread it around.

"I trust you, Father, that you know what's best for me. My heart aches a little sometimes, like tonight, and I still desire to share my life with someone, well... with James, actually. But if you'll just keep holding tight to me, Lord, I can get by without it, and it'll still be good because I'm with you. Just please hold tight and don't let me go."

Eighty-Five

Saturday
September 12

James was dreaming of the mountain mist again, only this time he was sure he was not searching for Betty. There was something else out there in the fog, but strangely, he didn't feel anxious or desperate. He knew he would find it, and soon.

"Dad? Dad, wake up," Ethan's voice broke through.

"What?" James tried to pry his eyes open. With the challenge of negotiating slumber on the waiting room's rock hard chairs, he had only nodded off an hour or so earlier. "Is it Grace?"

"She's still fine," Ethan assured him, "but things are starting to move along a little faster now. Doc says we might have a baby in three or four hours!"

"Hot dog! That's great!" James exclaimed. He noticed then that Tom was still perched on a chair in the corner, but had roused up at the sound of their voices. Strange that the fellow was still here.

"Dad." Ethan pulled his attention back. "Will you pray with me for Grace and the baby?"

Bowing his head, he saw Tom doing the same. That was something, anyway.

Surprisingly, James was able to doze off again and, not wanting to wake him, Nan and Tom had gone to the hospital cafeteria for breakfast without him. Stirring from his uncomfortable position around ten, he found he was completely famished and took himself off to find some food and drink, leaving Tom alone in the waiting area.

Accustomed as he was to Clare's and his own home-cooked fare, he found the hospital cuisine disappointing but filling. He got a cup of coffee "to go" and, once back on the second floor, moseyed over to the nursery viewing window.

At the moment, there were only two infants in view. In a few hours, though, his grandchild would be lying there in one of those little beds. And soon, he would be allowed to hold that tiny new life in his own arms.

There was nothing to compare with that, he thought. The feel of an infant cuddled close against you. It had been a long time since he and Betty had shared those moments, that special time of wonder and love radiating around a newborn baby and its parents, but he remembered well the joy he'd felt, both then and in the years that followed, though most of those years he had spent separated from his wife and his son.

Perhaps this time, if it was God's will, he would be allowed the privilege of watching his grandchild grow from infancy to adulthood! He could be a part of all the milestones, as well as all those precious, supposedly inconsequential, moments in this child's life. And maybe, just maybe, in sharing himself, he could impart something of value to that child. He hoped so.

Slowly, taking his time and talking to the staff along the way, he ambled back to the waiting room. He was surprised to see Clare, apparently deep in conversation with Tom, for she never even noticed when James entered the room. Nan was talking to Ethan near the door so he joined the two of them.

"Any news?" he asked.

Ethan grinned. "Not much longer now."

"They're getting her ready to go to the delivery room!" shared Nan.

James cried, "All right!" loudly enough that the two in the corner stopped talking to see what all the hubbub was about.

Eighty-Six

Gently, Ethan drew the receiving blanket down and gazed at his daughter's face. "She's beautiful, Grace."

"Yes." Grace could scarcely speak, there were so many emotions swirling deep in her heart. "D'you want to hold her?"

He nodded and held out his hands, uncertain quite where to place them, but figuring it out as he went. He caught his breath and watched intently as the baby's mouth pursed and fluttered. Tucking his finger inside the baby's fist, he grinned at Grace when the tiny fingers tightened around it. "This is awesome!"

"Yeah," she agreed. "What do you want to name her, Ethan?"

"Whatever you want, honey."

"Well…" she hesitated. "I was thinking…What about naming her after your mother? Wasn't her given name Elizabeth?"

Ethan looked up. "Yes. I'd love that. Dad would, too, I'm sure."

"We could call her Betty. Or there are lots of other nicknames for Elizabeth. And then, I'd like for her middle name to be Anne, after my Granny Annie. How do you feel about that?"

He tried it out. "'Elizabeth Anne'. That's nice. 'Betty Anne'. I like it." He brought the baby down close to Grace, so that their faces were close together. "How do you like your new name, Elizabeth Anne? You like it? I do, too." He kissed the infant's forehead. "Thank you for this beautiful daughter, Grace." He leaned over and softly kissed his wife.

"You're welcome," she smiled back. "But I think you had a little something to do with it too, dear."

Eighty-Seven

"So Tom and I are going back to Fairmount, I'm going to pack some clothes for Nan, then he's going to drive them back up here to her," Clare was explaining to James.

It didn't make sense to him, but he wasn't going to question their arrangements. He had more important things to do, like not missing his turn at holding that brand new baby girl.

Clare continued, "Are you staying a while longer, James?"

"What? Oh, yes, I'm going to stay until around five, I think. And, as you were just saying, Nan's going to stay the night, and Ethan's going home sometime later this evening. We'll both be back in the morning though."

She placed her hand on his arm and squeezed. "Isn't that baby girl the most precious thing you've ever laid eyes on?"

He patted her hand where it lay on his arm and unexpectedly didn't want to let go. She seemed to be looking at him in a most intimate way and their eyes locked for a moment. Why couldn't it be him instead of Tom, he thought. Reluctantly, he removed his hand and forced his eyes away.

"Precious, yes," he agreed, then walked away, down the hall and away from the source of the pain in his heart.

Eighty-Eight

When the phone rang, Clare was halfway through washing the supper dishes. Drying her hands, she hobbled into the hall to pick up the phone, thinking it might be Nan or Grace, giving her a final report on everyone's status for the night.

"Hello?" she said expectantly.

"Miss Morgan?" said a deep unfamiliar voice.

"Yes?"

"This is Bo Lucas, ma'am. Can I speak to Preacher James?"

"He's not here," she said, then corrected herself. "Actually, he doesn't live here anymore. He's finished with the mountain house, and he moved up there just a couple of days ago."

"Oh." Bo was silent for a few seconds. "I really need to talk to him. It's kind of urgent. Does he have a phone up there?"

"No, they're supposed to run the line next week. What is it, Bo? Do you want me to give him a message? I'm going to see him tomorrow."

Bo grunted. "That might be too late. Miss Morgan, you've got to get the word to him tonight."

This sounded ominous. "All right, Bo. I'll reach him somehow. What do I need to tell him?"

"Tell him... that Darrell Woody just told me that his daddy, Gus, is mad as the dickens at Preacher James for ratting him out about the fires. He's been hiding out for about a week, but he's coming for the Preacher tonight. He says he's going to kill him."

Clare hung up the phone and called Ethan's house. He was supposed to be coming home tonight. Maybe he was already there. But the answering machine picked up. Clare left a detailed message, passing on everything Bo had said, but that didn't solve her more immediate problem.

She called the sheriff's office and talked to the officer on duty. He was sympathetic, but because they only kept one deputy working the evening and night shift, there was no justification for him to sit and wait at James' house all night, based on nothing more than a tip that something might happen. He had to be available to serve the whole county as needed.

Though she didn't want to upset Grace or Nan, Clare had no choice but to call the hospital next. She asked Grace about the baby first, then asked to speak to Ethan. At Grace's request, he had gone to do some shopping in Gainesville before driving home to Fairmount. Grace guessed it might be another hour or so before he got back to the parsonage. Tom and Nan had just left to go out to eat.

What was she going to do? The only boarders she had at the moment were retired folks, and one young lady. Hardly the types she could ask to march into a potentially dangerous situation.

There was nothing for it but to go herself. She had a baseball bat in her bedroom closet that a tenant had left years ago, and right now she was darn glad she still had it. Grabbing her car keys, the bat and one crutch, she limped out the door with as much speed as she could muster. Halfway to the car she gave up on the crutch, and hopped along on the cast. She would worry about the doctor's orders tomorrow. Tonight, James was in trouble and she had to get to him.

Eighty-Nine

He'd been afraid he might fall asleep while driving home, he was that tired. James couldn't remember the last time he had gotten less than three hours sleep. Those waiting room chairs were more uncomfortable than the concrete benches they had in prison! But finally, he was home – albeit a little later than he had planned – and his intentions were to take a shower and go straight to bed.

He fumbled with the keys as he walked toward the house. Until Gus Woody stirred up all that ruckus he'd felt perfectly safe leaving his doors unlocked all the time, but now... Well, now he felt vulnerable unless he locked them at night and any time he was away from the house. It was a crying shame, but that was the way things were.

His shoes clumped across the front porch in the dark. There was no moon and he had left no porch lights on yesterday when he left in the middle of the day. He felt around for the lock and slid the house key in. James turned the knob, pushed the door open and walked in. That was the last thing he remembered.

Ninety

His head hurt like the devil though he couldn't think why, maybe because his brain seemed all scrambled up. He wanted to lift his hand and rub his temple, but for some reason he couldn't move his arm. He grimaced and tried to raise the other arm. Not possible.

Chin resting on his chest, he could feel something warm and wet dribbling down the right side of his face. In a detached way, he reasoned that perhaps it was connected to the throbbing in his temple.

Sounds began to filter in to his consciousness. There was at least one other person in the room with him. Recognizing the fresh lumber smell from all the renovations, he realized where he was. What was going on?

Before he could ponder that question, an iron grip twisted his head up as a rough voice bellowed right in his face, "Wake up, Holy-Roller! It's time to pay for your sins!"

James recognized the voice and the attitude, and knew he was in trouble. The smell of liquor was overwhelming which meant Gus was probably stinking drunk. Drunk and mean was a dangerous combination.

Gus continued his tirade. "May as well open your eyes, 'cause you're gonna want to see what I'm doing to ya'." When James didn't respond, Gus slapped him. Once, twice, three times. James forced himself to remain limp. He surmised that once Gus had James as an attentive audience, things would probably get out of control, but that as long as he didn't have an audience, he would soon lose interest.

He was right. Muttering to himself, Gus moved off toward the kitchen and opened the refrigerator door.

Taking advantage of his captor's momentary preoccupation, James forced his eyes open. His arms were held down tightly against the arms of the chair with duct tape. He checked to see if there was any "give" there, but there wasn't. Cautiously he raised his head, first locating Gus who was leaning into the freezer apparently looking for something to eat, then scouring the room for anything that could possibly enable his escape.

Ninety-One

Usually an excellent driver, Clare had run off the edge of the road three times and almost lost control on one of the mountain road's tight curves. Now she was talking to herself out loud.

"It's all right. It's all right. You're almost there. Everything's going to be fine. James is fine. He's up there in his house right now, drinking a Pepsi and eating a Moonpie. Calm down, Clare. Calm down. Almost there. Just a mile to go."

She happened to look down at the gas gauge. Sitting on empty. Aw, shoot! She had meant to fill up when she got back from the hospital, but she was running late, had to stop at the grocery, then rush home to have supper ready by six. Now look what a mess she'd made!

About that time she felt the motor "chug, chug" a couple of times, and the car began to slow. Furious with herself, she pulled off the side of the road and turned off the ignition. Foot! She threw her head down in her hands and started to bawl.

Then in her mind she saw James, the man she still loved with all her heart, alone and unprepared to face that devil Woody. A steely determination took over. She wasn't about to let anything happen to that man. Not if she could do anything to stop it. Wiping her eyes on her sleeves, she got out of the car, threw the bat over her shoulder and started up the mountain.

Ninety-Two

Still looking for a way to get loose, James considered trying to stand up, with the chair still attached. But what would he do then? It wasn't a very promising plan, but at the moment it was the only one he had. Gus had now moved from the refrigerator to the kitchen cabinets, pulling out boxes and cans and throwing them down on the floor, still not aware that James was awake.

Looking around the room again, James' gaze happened to scan the living room windows just as someone's shadow moved across the yard. No matter who it was, he didn't want anybody walking unaware into this unpredictable situation. He needed to warn them somehow, without tipping Gus off. Time to put on a show.

"Excuse me. Gus?" James was shouting, using his best and loudest "hell-fire and damnation" voice, the voice that could carry to the back row of a huge auditorium.

Startled, Gus whirled around, dropping the can of pork'n'beans he was holding straight down on his left big toe. That was the same toe in which he had suffered a bout of the gout for the last several days, the very tender, sore toe which had caused him to replace the fancy cowboy boots he usually wore with a cheap pair of men's house shoes, which of course provided no protection at all to his swollen sore toe from a free-falling one pound can of pork'n'beans.

As the can rolled away into the dining room, Gus swayed on his feet, his eyes crossing in pain. Then, his knees buckling, he fell to the floor and gently picked up his foot, cradling it in his hands, moaning, cursing loudly and rocking back and forth.

James was so astonished by the drama in front of him, that he ceased his efforts at creating a distraction. Apparently, it wasn't going to be necessary. Anyone within a mile of here could hear the caterwauling spewing forth from Gus' mouth.

Ninety-Three

Outside in the dark, Clare was watching and listening. She saw James taped into the chair and Gus cussing like a drunken sailor on the floor. So much for warning James in time, she thought. As she stared through the window from her hiding place in the bushes, she saw Gus take his shoe off and examine the toe. Even from her vantage point, the toe looked like one of those red hot sausages, bright red and swollen. Oooh. She squeezed her eyes shut. She didn't want to see that.

But the wailing stopped and she had to look. The pain must have eased up, for Gus put his shoe back on and stood up, gingerly putting his weight on that foot. The look in his eyes was pure madness and - when he turned toward James - murderous.

Gus was going to kill him. Clare knew that, just as sure as she knew that she loved James MacEwen with every fiber of her being. She had to do something.

Should she go to the nearest neighbor for help? Get to a phone and call the sheriff? Clare had a bad feeling – that there was not enough time, that something terrible would happen before she could navigate half a mile back down the mountain. The decision made, she shifted the bat in her hand and got a better grip.

Around to the back of the house she crept. Twice she had come to view the progress on the house, so she knew there were two doors leading into the house from the back porch. As quietly as possible she went toward the end of the house where the bedrooms were located.

When she rounded the corner of the new bathroom, a protruding pipe caught her right across the shinbone of her uninjured leg and she had to grab her mouth to stifle the howl she couldn't quite hold back. She stood still and listened.

Nothing. She didn't know if that was a good sign or a bad sign. Regardless, she'd better hurry.

She felt around until she found the steps leading up to the back porch, and practically crawled up them. Once on the porch, she got to her feet and hunched way over, on the off chance that Gus might be able to see her outline through the window of the door leading to the kitchen.

Sliding her feet carefully across the porch, she held her hands out in front, feeling her way across the outside wall. When her hand passed over the door frame, instead of touching a closed door her right hand swished through empty air. The door was open!

Ninety-Four

When Gus stood up and began moving toward him, glaring and baring his yellowed teeth, James figured it was time to start talking.

"Gus, listen to me. We can work this out..."

Gus lunged toward him and roared, "Shut up, preacher man. I'm fixin' to kill you and I'm gonna enjoy doin' it!" He began to circle around James, yelling, "You ratted me out to the law!" and "It's over now. You're as good as dead." He punctuated each outburst by whacking James in the head with his open palm.

"Gus, you don't have to do this. I forgive you."

"Well, I don't forgive you." Gus ran his arm along the mantel, sending picture frames crashing to the hearth."

"It's not too late to turn things around in your life." James pleaded with him.

Gus came close and got right in James' face. "Like you turned my boy around?" he sneered. "Like you turned him against me?" He circled James again, then again.

The dining room chair in which James was tied up was facing away from the fireplace so that he had a clear view into the hall. He saw a movement near the bedroom door. Someone was coming to help him.

The next time Gus was between him and the hall, James was determined to gain his full attention.

"Gus?" he said, in his most compelling voice. "I didn't mean to come between you and your boy. Were you close?"

Gus struck a pose. "Of course we was close. We done everything together. Drank beer. Went fishin'. Stole a wallet or two. Beat up a few people, anybody that messed with us." He drew back his fist and punched James in the eye. "Like that."

His eye was already swelling, he could feel it, but he had to keep Gus talking. He could see the shadow of his rescuer behind Gus, coming ever closer. "I've got a son, Gus. We're close, too, so I understand what you're talking about." With his good eye he glanced past Gus.

Oh, no. It was Clare.

Ninety-Five

Clare thought for a minute that she was home free, so to speak. She made it down the hall undetected, and had covered the distance across the living room to within a few feet of where Gus stood. But then James saw her, and the expression on his face must have given her away.

She already had the bat drawn back, poised to knock the stew out of old Gus, when that scoundrel whipped around and with one swipe of that big bear claw of a hand sent her flying across the room, the bat clattering on the wooden floor.

As she was sailing through the air, with a stroke of genius it occurred to her that pretending to be unconscious might be a smart thing to do right now, so she forced herself to take the fall without breaking it in any way, and to lay sprawled out however she happened to land. Gus was just inebriated enough that he fell for it.

When she was a child, she had been an expert at closing her eyes almost completely, but keeping them open a tiny slit, just enough to look between her lashes and see whatever there was to see. What she saw now was Gus, continuing to watch her, not letting his guard down. Not yet, she thought, but he will.

In the rare moments when he looked away, she searched her line of vision for the baseball bat. It had rolled under the desk. Not much chance of retrieving it, it was too far away. He would catch her before she could use it. Surely there was something else within her reach that she could use as a weapon.

Gus had knocked her toward the kitchen area where debris from his foraging was scattered all over the floor. In fact she was pretty sure she was lying on top of some canned goods. Extremely uncomfortable, canned goods.

There were cans of chili and pork'n'beans, boxes of pasta, and tins of sardines, Vienna sausage, potted meat and Spam. Good grief, is that all the man ate, up here all by himself? Clare was appalled. That issue would have to wait however. At the moment she was supposed to be looking for a weapon. Then she spotted it.

A medium sized cast iron frying pan. It was barely beyond her reach, just above her head. She watched Gus closely and when she saw her chance, she inched up a little closer and snagged the frying pan.

Ninety-Six

James was aching, not from his injuries, but with fear for Clare. She was so still, he thought she might already be dead. The thought crushed him. He hadn't even told her how he felt.

Gus was on a rampage now. His eyes were glittering like those of a madman and he seemed even more agitated than before. James didn't like the way he was looking at Clare either.

"You know what I think I'm gonna do next, Preacher? 'Course it's all gonna end up the same way, with me killing you, but I think we should make it a little more interesting than me just killing you straight out."

As Gus was talking, James could see in his peripheral vision minute movements from Clare. He was relieved, but concerned that she might again try something foolish.

"Don't you think so, Preacher? Well then, I tell you what I'm gonna do. First, I think I'll take that poker over there by the fireplace, and I'll poke your eyes out."

James saw Clare reach for something and grab hold of it.

Gus continued with his threats. "Nope! Hold up, I can't poke your eyes out just yet. First, I'm gonna have my way with that woman over there, and you need your eyes to see that, don't you, Preacher?"

James could see Clare slowly rising. Not wanting to thwart her efforts again, he kept his eyes set firmly on Gus.

"Whadya say, man? Wanna see me "do my thing" with that slut over there?"

Keep him talking, keep him looking at me, thought James. Lord, protect Clare, please. "Come on, Gus. Don't do these things. It's never too late to change your life." Just another couple of feet, Clare.

"I don't want to change my life. See, that's what you preacher-types don't understand. I'm perfectly happy the way I am. I like being bad."

Clare drew back the frying pan and pounded it down on Gus's big toe. When he bent double in pain to grab it, she swung again and whacked him on the back of the head. He crumpled to the floor, out cold.

She threw the skillet down and her hand flew to her mouth. "Aw, James, he hurt you," she whimpered, reaching out, but not touching him.

"Thank God, you're alive," he said. "I thought you were dead." He wanted to hold her, but his arms were still hampered.

She was pulling at the duct tape, trying to tear it loose.

"Use a knife. It'll be faster," he said. "And hurry. We don't want him to 'come to' until we have him tied up."

"Of course." She ran to the kitchen, got the knife and cut him loose.

As soon as he was free, James went out on the back porch and came back with a length of thick rope. Kneeling down, he tied Gus's hands tightly behind him. "How did you know to come?" he asked, as she helped him bind the rope around Gus's legs and ankles.

"Bo called the boarding house looking for you. Darrell said his daddy was coming tonight to kill you."

James breathed a prayer of thanks. "Thank you, Father, for watching over me tonight."

"Amen, amen. Thank you," she echoed. They were both still kneeling on the floor. He stood up then held out his hand to help her to her feet. They were standing close together, just looking at each other, not moving. James' lips parted, whether to say something important that needed to be said, or to kiss her, he wasn't sure, but either way, it never came to pass.

Ethan came bursting through the door, and the opportunity was lost.

Ninety-Seven

Monday
September 14

"Easy now. Take your time, sweetheart." Like a honey bee bumbling from one blossom to another, Ethan was buzzing around Grace and the infant she held in her arms, anxious to make their homecoming as perfect as humanly possible.

The back door opened and Nan and Clare came rushing out to usher them in. Through all the hullaballoo of "oohs" and "ahhhs" and passing the infant around so that everyone had a turn, little Betty Anne slept on, peaceful and serene.

Finally, Grace was settled on the couch holding the infant, Ethan snuggled up close, with his hand resting on the baby's head. Clare had her arm around Nan's shoulder as they stood in the doorway taking in the sweet scene.

Not to disturb the young couple, she spoke softly to her friend. "I'm going to miss you, staying at the boarding house with me. You won't forget to come and visit, will you?"

"Of course not," Nan whispered back. "I'll be over all the time! You know Miss Independent won't want me underfoot but just so much."

Clare giggled. "Yeah, I forgot about that." They stood in silence, enjoying the shared moment with loved ones.

Then Clare straightened up. "I've got to go. Duty calls! There's plenty of food, all you have to do is warm it up."

"You're a treasure, my friend," Nan answered as she hugged her. Quietly, Clare waved goodbye and tiptoed away, leaving the four of them in blissful tranquility.

Ninety-Eight

Alone in the nursery with the sleeping child, Grace picked up the Baby Journal. On the first page she had written a title: "In the Beginning: The First Seven Days with Betty Anne".

She flipped over a few pages and began to write.

"Day Three. We're home now. Betty Anne is sleeping for the first time in her own little bed. Her daddy has gone to the church to catch up on his preacher work since he's been otherwise occupied with more important things for the last few days."

Rising from the rocker, Grace leaned over the crib, making sure Betty Anne was still breathing. As she watched, the tiny chest rose and fell. Reassured, Grace resumed her writing.

"I am watching my baby sleep. She's so beautiful, it hurts. Imagining what her life will be like is too big a thought for me, so I guess I'll just have to watch it unfold as it happens.

"I do know that she will be surrounded by love. Her father and I will always be there for her. Her grandfather James is so in love with her already, he would hold her from now 'til forever if I would let him. And my mom, whom Betty Anne will probably call "Nana", tears up every time she holds her in her arms, she's just so happy that Betty Anne is here with us.

"Lots of 'firsts' today. First time in her own bed. First time at home with Momma and Daddy. First time for Daddy to change her diaper. First time to fall asleep in Daddy's arms. First time for Nana to rock her.

I have a feeling that from now on, every day with Betty Anne is going to be filled with lots of "firsts". Life is going to be one big continuous surprise. I can't wait!"

Ninety-Nine

Thursday
September 17

"Lawzy-mercy, I can't even recollect how many years it's been since I've seen this view." Miss Sally was sitting in a rocker on James' back porch, obviously enjoying her promised visit to his home.

"I guess you visited Miss Sadie when she lived here?" he asked, drawing up a chair to sit beside her.

"Oh, my, yes! Sadie and me were always thick as thieves." She pointed to the left, down the hill from the porch. "Every summer we picked blackberries right down there. Folks said my blackberry jelly was the best on the mountain." Then she pointed her knobby finger off to the right. "And there was a tremendous honey tree straight down that way, close to where the branch runs through this property. We used to harvest the honey once a year. My Harold always did that for us," she said proudly. "You know, Beamon never did anything unless it was slick and underhanded."

"I remember," said James.

She went on, "Did you know Harold and Beamon used to make 'shine together?"

"No, I never heard about that."

"Well, they did. Got caught, too. At least Harold did. Revenooers found him and the still back up in the holler above our house. That was in 1923."

"What happened to Harold?"

"Oh, they put him in the penitentiary," said Sally. "For ten years. Loneliest years of my life, they was. I was never so happy to see anybody as I was to see my Harold the day he got home."

"I can't imagine."

Miss Sally turned and looked sternly at James. "Yes, you can imagine, Brother James. Prison took a part of your life, too."

He nodded in agreement. "Yes, ma'am, you're right."

She picked back up where she left off. "Harold missed me something awful, too. That prison changed him some, but not where most folks could tell. I could tell, though."

James waited for her to go on. When she didn't, he asked, "Did it harden him?"

She answered quickly, "Oh, no. Not Harold. It just made him appreciate everything, like he never did before. He was the most grateful man you've ever seen." She turned and smiled sweetly. "Reminds me a lot of you, Preacher."

One Hundred

Saturday
September 19

These days, James just couldn't seem to stay away from that parsonage. Of course, he knew it had everything to do with the fact that the parsonage was where his precious, adorable, immeasurably sweet baby granddaughter lived.

Every day, he set aside time to stop by and spend at least a few minutes holding her, and if she happened to be awake, whispering sweet nothings in her ear. Today, he had the whole afternoon open and was planning to stay at least a couple of hours.

He was surprised to see Tom's black Camaro parked in the driveway when he arrived. The last he heard, Tom had returned to New York, though James had always assumed he would be back in Fairmount as soon as he had made the arrangements for Clare to join him. Maybe he and Clare had come over to visit.

He knocked on the back door, softly in case the baby was sleeping, then stuck his head in. Nan was just coming to answer the door.

"Hi, James." She hugged his neck. "Come on in. We're in the den." She led the way through the kitchen. "Grace and Ethan have gone out for lunch. She said she was going to have some of that chicken salad she didn't get to eat last week!"

The first thing James saw when he entered the den was Tom, holding *his* granddaughter. Stifling his initial feeling of jealousy, he managed a civil greeting. "Where's Clare?" he asked.

Nan answered, "She's at the boarding house, but she's coming over later."

With an understanding smile, Tom gestured toward the infant asleep in his arms. "James, do you want to hold her?"

Swallowing any pride he might have had left, James nodded, then grinned. "Yes, I sure do!" He gathered up the baby and her blankets from Tom and settled himself on the sofa.

"Well, while the baby is happy, and you two gents seem to have things under control, I'm going to fix some sandwiches. James, have you had lunch?"

He tore his eyes away from the bundle he was holding. "No, not really. But, if it's any trouble…"

"Gosh, no. We're still trying to eat up all the food folks have brought. Please, eat something!" Nan begged.

"Okay. Whatever you're having is fine," said James.

"Ham sandwiches. Tom, mayo and lettuce?"

"That's how I like it," he confirmed.

"James?" she asked.

"Mayonnaise and mustard, please."

"Good enough. It'll be ready in a few minutes," said Nan, leaving the men to themselves.

James would have been perfectly happy to sit in silence, but Tom seemed to want to talk. "I've not been around babies much. Have you?"

"Only Ethan. But that was a long time ago."

"Nan has certainly been excited about her first grandchild. First grandchild for you, too."

James agreed, "It's pretty special."

There was a pause as Tom seemed to search for something more to say. "I heard about the incident up at your place with that crazy guy, Gus…what was his name?"

"Gus Woody."

"Ah. Sounded like a horrific experience."

James thought, Clare must have filled him in on all the details. "Yes, pretty disturbing. I probably wouldn't be sitting here right now holding my granddaughter if it weren't for Clare."

"She is fairly amazing, isn't she?"

"Yes, she is," James agreed. "So, you're back from New York. How long do you think you'll stay in Fairmount?"

"Actually, I haven't made it well-known yet, but I plan to be in Fairmount a good bit from now on, perhaps spend half of the year here."

"Oh. Well, I guess Clare is happy about that."

"Oh, yes. She and I were able to work it out splendidly. We were both quite pleased with the arrangement."

"Well. I'm happy for you both," said James, in all sincerity. "Will you live at the boarding house while you're here?"

"For a few months anyway. That was part of the arrangement. Then, I'll want to purchase my own house."

"Will Clare continue to run the boardinghouse?"

Tom looked surprised that he would ask. "Of course. Why wouldn't she?"

James shrugged. "I just thought...Well, what about when you're living in New York? Won't she travel to New York with you?"

"Nan?"

"No," said James, wondering why Nan's name had even come up. "I'm talking about Clare."

Tom seemed perplexed as he tried to explain. "After we get married.....? Nan will travel with me to New York."

"You mean Clare."

Tom shook his head. "No. I mean Nan. After Nan and I get married, we'll travel back and forth from Fairmount to New York."

Now James was totally confused. "You're marrying Nan? What about the arrangements you made with Clare?"

"For two rooms at the boarding house. My living quarters upstairs and an office downstairs. You mean you thought Clare and I....?" Tom began to chuckle. "Oh, my word! That certainly explains a lot of things!"

"So you and Clare are not together?"

"Oh, good heavens, no! It was clear to both of us almost immediately that there was no spark between us. We're friends and will always be just that."

At that moment, Nan bustled in, loaded down with a tray filled with sandwiches and glasses of milk. "Okay, boys, I'll take the baby and you can chow down."

James readily transferred the little bundle into her waiting arms. He looked from one to the other, unable to keep from smiling even as he said, "I'm not going to be able to stay for lunch. I'm sorry, please excuse me." Still smiling, he hurried on his way.

"What's going on?" Nan wanted to know. "Where is he going in such a hurry?"

Tom smiled and winked at his fiancée. "I believe the good preacher needs to make some arrangements."

"Oh. What kind of arrangements?"

"For a wedding."

Nan tilted her head at Tom, a question in her eyes.

He nodded in confirmation.

"Ohhhh, *that* wedding!" She cradled Betty Anne in her arms and danced her slowly around the room, coming back to rest within Tom's arms, her head against his shoulder.

One Hundred One

At the back door of the boarding house James stopped, his hand on the doorknob. He could see her, the love of his heart, through the window. The radio was blaring and Clare was singing along as she washed dishes, swaying to the music. Her single crutch was leaned against the counter close by. As the music reached its peak, she laid her head back and let it fly, her voice swelling through the high notes, then cutting short suddenly as she stopped to scrub a rough spot on a frying pan.

Please, Lord, let her still love me, he prayed. He knocked on the window. She saw him and smiled, just as she always did. Motioning him to come in, she grabbed a dish towel and dried her hands.

"Hey, Stranger! I thought you'd be at Grace and Ethan's holding that precious baby girl some more."

"I just came from there," he said.

"Oh. Well, what are you up to now?"

He moved a step or two closer. "Actually, I was hoping you had time to go for a drive with me. Up to the mountain house."

"Right now?" she said, obviously bemused.

"Yeah. Right now."

"This is important to you." It was more a statement than a question.

"Yes. Can you come?" He held his breath.

"Sure," she said. "I'll be ready in a jiffy."

The ride up the mountain was pleasant, though they didn't talk much. The higher they went, the more nervous James became. He began to have misgivings and doubts about the whole situation. Perhaps he should have given this more thought and planning. After all, he was about to propose marriage to a woman whom he'd never even asked out on a date before. Maybe it wasn't fair to put Clare on the spot like this. Finally he concluded that whatever happened, it was all in his Father's hands.

When they came to a stop at the house, he ran around the truck to help her out with her crutch. She actually managed very well on her own and hardly needed his help, but he offered her his hand anyway and she took it.

It was a perfect September day, sunny and just warm enough. It had rained the day before so the air was very clean and fresh, and even the far off mountains could be seen clearly. It was a lovely day to woo a woman.

James led her around the house to the porch and held her elbow as she navigated the steps using her crutch. There was a new porch swing he had painted and hung the week before. She sat down in it, laying her crutch to the side. He took his place beside her. She looked at him expectantly, waiting.

"Clare, I owe you an apology," he began. "You shared your feelings with me when we were in the truck one night, and I didn't give you any response at all."

"It's okay, James, I...."

"Please. Let me say what I need to say. I didn't answer you because I panicked. I couldn't get the words out. And then I was too embarrassed afterwards.

"The truth is, there were some things in my past that I needed to face before I could consider a relationship with anyone. So, I've been working on those issues and I've made some headway. A few weeks ago I realized that I did have feelings for you but that something was holding me back.

"And this is what it was: Deep down, I knew I wasn't good enough for you. With the unseemly life I've had, I couldn't be worthy of someone like you."

Clare had heard enough. "Unworthy of me? Not good enough for me? How could you ever think such a thing? Let's put aside for the moment your intelligence and your appearance and your talents. James, you are the finest man I've ever known. You endured a tragic, devastating blow, with your life in shackles most of your adult life. Yet you came through that fire with grace, and without bitterness or resentment..."

"But I have been resentful," he broke in. "On the inside anyway. I had more or less accepted everything back when I was in prison. But when I got out... I didn't even realize it or maybe I didn't want to admit it, but I have resented missing thirty years of my life. Especially the time I should have been caring for Betty and Ethan.

"But that's one of the things My Father and I are going to keep working on. He's shown it to me and I recognize it now, so I can begin to deal with it and He can heal it.

"But there's something else, Clare." He took a deep breath to steady himself. "Even though my mind tells me otherwise, I feel... I feel a sense of shame that I've been in prison most of my life. I... you're getting damaged goods. There's no way for me to change the reality of the life I've lived.…..

Clare's fingers touched his lips. "Shhhh... The life you've lived has made you who you are, just as mine has made me who I am. I've got flaws and imperfections, too." She held out her arms, hands open-faced in front of her. "I'm just a plain old mountain girl. Never been anywhere or done anything big or exciting. Just cooked and cleaned my whole life." She looked straight at him, unashamed, and softly murmured, "But I do love you, James MacEwen."

James was staring fixedly at the vista spread out in front of them. Tears rolled down his cheeks, but he never moved or said a word.

Finally, she realized that he needed just a little help over that last bump in the road. Favoring her injured ankle, she carefully pulled herself across the seat of the swing to settle into his lap. She wiped the tears away and turned his head to face her.

"What do you think, James? Is there a place in your life for a simple mountain girl? Is there room for me?"

Slowly, ever so slowly, as if dark clouds were rolling away to be replaced little by little with patches of sunlight, his expression changed. Relief shone in his eyes and his face lit up with joy as he spoke. "Oh, yes. I'm making a place for you, Clare. A great big comfortable spot for you, right here beside me." His arms went around and rocked her in a warm hug. "And right here in my heart."

He lifted her chin and kissed her tentatively. But that wasn't enough. Grabbing her up in his arms, he stood and twirled her around in circles on the wide porch, and Clare threw back her head and laughed in unabashed joy. As he gradually slowed, he let go of her legs and eased her feet down until she was standing on her own. Then he kissed her, thoroughly and well.

When the kiss ended, they were breathing hard and staring into each other's eyes with tenderness and wonder and thankfulness.

As James pulled her close again, he whispered, "I love you, Clare Morgan. Let's spend the rest of our lives together, my dear mountain girl. Shall we?"

Epilogue

The fog was thick on the mountain this morning. It had settled lightly the night before, down in all the hidden hollers and in the scraggly tree branches, then it had thickened, like bean broth thickens when you cook it long enough. Every surface was damp with it, the ground and the leaves and the grass and the tree bark. Even the tombstones were wet and slick with it.

James had been here for a while. He was remembering the long ago days, when he was young, when he danced with Betty and made flower chains and played hide and seek in the piney woods. The memories were so very old, they were beginning to fade a little. But they were still very lovely.

In his dreams he had lost her in the fog and the mist. He had searched for her, grasping at the wisps, his fingers sliding through and touching only the damp air. He had become tired from never finding his true love. So very tired.

He thought for a moment he heard her calling still, but she was gone from this world. He turned away.

There it was again. The voice of his love, coming to him, growing ever closer. He couldn't see her through the fog but he knew in his heart that she was there, waiting only for him.

She called to him and he took a step toward her. She called again and he began to run.

Through the fog, the light bore down, breaking through, separating the tufts, drawing the strands apart, glowing, shining through their translucence, lighting the way for him through the mist.... until at last he saw her.

His love, dressed in white for their marriage this morning.

His Clare, standing at the steps of Heaven's Mountain Church, waiting for him.

At last he saw her. His own dear mountain girl.

Dedication

In loving memory of my dear friend Lisa Ashlock Turner, a genuine mountain girl from the hills of Tennessee and the real-life inspiration for the character of Clare, who appears in all three books of the Heaven's Mountain trilogy.

In the first book, when Clare Morgan became a literary persona, it was Lisa's voice I heard in my head as I wrote Clare's dialogue and it was her personality that was the starting point for Clare's character. I never imagined that within a few years I would no longer get to hear that merry voice speak of "packing" (carrying) something, or laughing with me over something silly.

Lisa found joy and laughter in all the little things in life, and she was generous in sharing that joy with every person she passed along the way, no exceptions. That girl had an amazing gift -the ability to make every person she met feel like they were special and they were worth something.

Sometimes when you saw Lisa, she would have on her "work clothes", just anything she could find, which might or might not match, and then other times, she absolutely sparkled on the outside and glowed from the inside, she would be just that radiant with beauty and joy.

She loved to make her home shine with beauty and warmth, too, with homey touches and flowers everywhere. She made everyone who came in the yard or walked through the door feel welcome, and as if they were coming home.

Her faith was simple and absolute. It was always there and she spoke of it in the most natural way, never condescending or self-righteous or preachy, but real and genuine and down to earth. She lived her faith, too, by being kind and generous and hospitable not just to the more appealing people, but to the unappealing, the poor, the misfits that most of us tend to ignore. Without meaning to, she frequently made me feel ashamed of myself, for not treating people as generously and lovingly as she did.

I heard her say many times, "If you want to have a friend, you need to be a friend". Lisa truly knew how to do that. She was a wonderful friend to me and to many others.

Whenever it was time to leave, Lisa always gave a hug and said "I love you", as if she wanted to be sure, no matter what happened between the times we were together, we would always know that she loved us.

Until I see you again in heaven, dear friend….

Made in the USA
Columbia, SC
25 May 2018